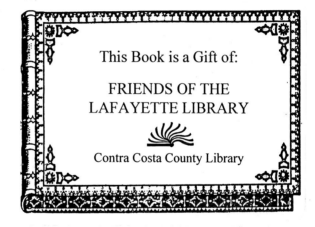

The Lighthouse, the Cat, and the Sea

Also by Leigh W. Rutledge

If People Were Cats
Diary of a Cat
Dear Tabby
Cat Love Letters
A Cat's Little Instruction Book

A Tropical Tale

Leigh W. Rutledge

THE
LIGHTHOUSE,
THE CAT,
AND THE SEA

DUTTON
Published by the Penguin Group
Penguin Putnam Inc., 375 Hudson Street, New York, New York 10014, U.S.A.
Penguin Books Ltd, 27 Wrights Lane, London W8 5TZ, England
Penguin Books Australia Ltd, Ringwood, Victoria, Australia
Penguin Books Canada Ltd, 10 Alcorn Avenue, Toronto, Ontario, Canada M4V 3B2
Penguin Books (N.Z.) Ltd, 182–190 Wairau Road, Auckland 10, New Zealand

Penguin Books Ltd, Registered Offices: Harmondsworth, Middlesex, England

First Published by Dutton, a member of Penguin Putnam Inc.

First Printing, October, 1999
10   9   8   7   6   5   4   3   2   1

 REGISTERED TRADEMARK—MARCA REGISTRADA

LIBRARY OF CONGRESS CATALOGING-IN-PUBLICATION DATA
Rutledge, Leigh W.
    The lighthouse, the cat, and the sea : a tropical tale / Leigh W. Rutledge.
        p.   cm.
    ISBN 0-525-94349-8 (alk. paper)
    1. Cats Fiction.   I. Title.
PS3568.U8238L54   1999
813' .54—dc21   99-25119
                                                                    CIP

Printed in the United States of America
Set in Goudy
Designed by Eve L. Kirch

To the memory of Legolas

The Sea

ONE

*O*h, when I think of the cats at sea on a night like this! The mousers and the captain's companions. The innocent stowaways huddled belowdecks, looking for a little warmth and a small dry niche—in a corner of the cargo hold or under the simple bed of a sailor—to rest their weary paws. Seeking free passage in the tradition of seafaring cats for hundreds of years, and bound on who-knows-what errands of infelicitous desperation. Tossed back and forth upon a tumultuous sea, as if the sea were a metaphor for everything a cat must endure in this life. I, for one, am glad to be safely home, by the fire, on a night such as this. And yet, I cannot help envying them a little—they who will spend this or any other night at sea. For being at sea is like being in love: There is little peace to it, but one is never more alive.

Call me Mrs. Moore—though why you should call me that I am not certain; the name was given to me long before I could add *my* counsel or consent. I certainly was *not* a kitten bride. Indeed, I have never been betrothed to anyone. So why I should be burdened all my life with a name denoting matrimony is a mystery to me.

I am an old cat now. I am thirty-one years old—an obscene age for a cat. An unconscionable, maddening age. What was God thinking? After all, it is His will that decides these things; I can claim no credit for my age. I have heard it suggested I may be the oldest living cat on the planet. Such a distinction! As if longevity—like intelligence or comeliness—were in itself desirable, or represented something beyond the mere capriciousness of Nature.

I sleep a great deal now, too much sleep—an appalling development for one who was once so spirited and meddlesome. There was a time I could hardly sleep at all for fear of missing one more tree to climb, one more bug to chase, or a set of draperies in need of removal from their rod. I was once too agitated, too charmed by the sheer variety of life's pleasures to sleep.

Now I sit. Alone. With my memories. Like the great Sphinx at

Giza. Or I lie in the grass, too weary even to swat at dragonflies that dance around my nose. How many times have I been lying in the grass this way, only to have some human come upon me— fearfully, worriedly—and remark when I suddenly opened my eyes, "Oh! I was afraid you were dead."

No, not yet. Not quite.

Sometimes I sit cozily among the garden flowers and listen to the songs of the sea wind, or to the soothing rumble of distant thunder. And I think of Fafner. And Señorita. The first mate. And the crew of the *Estella Gomez*. I am often haunted by the voices of those I have left behind. Sometimes I wander through the garden and imagine that I hear a distant meow, and think, "Oh, there's Mr. Peach come to call. Oh, there's Schooner with some bright, witty observation about the folly of the islanders," until I realize, with a pinch to my heart, that they are gone, really and truly.

But then, this is a haunted island. I knew it even when I was a kitten, that ghosts were drawn to this place and that those who have died here, in the middle of the emerald ocean, find it difficult to leave.

Two

*I*t is the vulgar habit of modern memoirs to begin by flaunting one's ancestry in the reader's face, thereby proving that the current fruit of the family tree is not only worth attention but represents an exciting climax to generations of enviable mating.

We have been, for as long as anyone can remember, a family of seafaring cats.

A celebrated aunt of mine sailed with the pirate Jean Lafitte aboard the frigate *Barataria Bay* in the early 1800s. She was Lafitte's constant companion, and seems to have had only one duty aboard ship: to chase the pirate's toes through his bedcovers at night and make him laugh when a long day of looting left him melancholy. Whether or not she, too, was a brigand at heart, I

cannot say, but she obviously loved her life on earth. To this day, her ghost haunts vessels approaching the port of New Orleans. I have sometimes considered a trip to Louisiana with the ambition of encountering her. However, given my own proximity to the hereafter, I am sure we shall meet soon enough.

Another member of our family traveled with Darwin on the H.M.S. *Beagle*, but impetuously devoured one of the naturalist's prize specimens, and was forced to decamp at Cape Foulwind, New Zealand. And a distant cousin (twice removed) is reputed to have sat at Shakespeare's side as the playwright sailed down the Thames and conceived the opening lines of *Henry IV*. My cousin is universally credited with having inspired the immortal line, "I am as melancholy as a gib cat."

But the majority of my antecedents were simple creatures. That they managed to survive hurricanes, wars, and pestilence for thousands of years is quite enough.

I think that too much emphasis is placed on the admiration of one's ancestors—as if they were a silver pot, or a diamond broach. If one claims kinship with the best of one's lineage, one must also be tied to the worst: the bores, the ones with bad breath. A family tree would have more use if one could actually climb it. Alas, too many creatures doze in its shadow.

THREE

I was born on the schooner *Estella Gomez* as it sailed the straits of Florida in the year 1899. The current and wind were with *Estella* when she broke anchor off the coast of Cuba that day, bound for Key Largo.

My mother was a ship's mouser, which is to say she had no hearth or berth to call her own, no generous hand to feed her table scraps at the end of a day or stroke her ears at night. Cargo holds of copra were her bedchamber; aromatic crates of spice and linen were her hideaways.

She lived her entire life aboard ship, amid the riggings and coconut rats and swaying hammocks of the crew. When she grew too loud in her pursuit of prey or had a rollicking encounter with the captain's dog, the crew threw an empty rum bottle at her and cursed the day she was born. Otherwise, she was answerable to no one. She had no name—and what in the end is more a symbol of exile from all that is tender in the world than to be nameless?

She was not a pretty cat. Indeed, she was quite skinny—emaciated—and very plain in the face; indistinguishable from the thousands of overworked cats kept on cargo ships in those days. It was almost certainly for the sake of expedience, not admiration, that any tom possessed her.

Of my father, I know nothing. Cats never do. It is part of our mystique and our tragedy. We are a fatherless species.

Oh, but the passage to Key Largo! What should have taken barely more than a day dragged on to two and then three. Halfway across the Straits, the crew encountered foul weather. The morning of my birth began with a reposing sea the color of pale blue opals, and *Estella* its serene mistress; by twilight, grim slate churned beneath the schooner's hull, and she began to spin and convulse like a hapless sampan. Great, foamy swells tormented her progress, and mountainous waves tumbled over her decks. The felon wind pilfered everything that was not lashed down—including one member of the crew (miraculously rescued two days later, clinging to a cask of beer).

It is said any creature born aboard ship during a violent storm is fated to have ill fortune in life. I can speak here only of my mother's misfortune in having gone into labor on turbulent seas. As the ship lurched forward on furied waves, my mother caterwauled with the burden of her maternal duty. Back and forth, the ship rolled, back and forth, until it seemed a certainty the vessel would overturn completely and be forced to sail upside down evermore, with its masts plunged in the murky deep and its keel pointed skyward. My mother sweated. She panted. She clawed at the timbers in anguish and confusion. All around her, crates and cartons tumbled in the darkness or were tossed through the air above her head. When, at last, we—her kittens—came into the world, it was at the peak of the disturbance. Expelled from her body, we tumbled like loose fittings across the bilge, and rolled halfway up the bulkhead.

Oh, those cats who whine and whimper over the privations of their pampered existence ashore! Dinner is late tonight, my pillows aren't properly fluffed, I'm *bored*—let them try a voyage at sea to cure their boredom and ease their indignation!

The shriek of the wind, the boom of thunder, the violence of giant waves, these attended *my* first blind feelings at my mother's nipples.

The Sea

And when, some ten days later, I opened my eyes for the first time and examined my new home, it was to discover that I had been born not into a life of comfort and predictability, of soft couch cushions and sunny windows, but rather a world of—limes.

FOUR

$\mathcal{G}$unshots and wailing. A clamor such as might have erupted from the citizens of Troy at the very instant the Greeks poured from their infamous horse and began the slaughter. Even the falcons and parrots over our heads seemed distraught.

Orders were bellowed in the blazing tropical sun: "Get out of the tree! Get out of it *now*, or we'll shoot!" A great cry—a hundred, two hundred voices at once—rose from the dock, full of rage, panic, and derisive laughter. Women began to sing; they mocked their attackers with *Oh, no sailors live in shantytown*. But gunshots quickly ended their ballad. The bullets struck not the singers, but the melody itself, and with it, all hope of reconciliation.

"Out of the lime tree! Out of the lime tree this instant!" another man's voice rose above the rest; but the mob, like a seething pool of mud, overwhelmed and drowned out his words with its shrieks and shouts and obscenities.

We were docked at Cayo Dulzura—the Island of Sweetness— 120 miles east of Havana. It was the sixteenth of August, nearly four weeks after my birth.

A riot was in progress.

An immense, sprawling lime tree grew dockside. Proudly. A hundred years old, at least. With its fat gray limbs, it called to mind a giant elephant. Multiple trunks careened skyward, thick as cannons. Taller than the tallest house: an exquisite thing, sparkling alive with jade-colored leaves and the purest yellow of the yellow Caribbean light. And it was, at that moment, so crowded with people on every branch and extremity, climbing, swinging, swaying, ascending, descending, clutching twigs for dear life, that for years afterward I lived with the delusion that this was how people were born: cultivated on trees like oversized fruit, until they ripened and plopped to the ground. There were a hundred, perhaps a hundred and fifty people in the tree.

The young and the elderly, every man, woman, and child struggled to fill every conceivable receptacle with limes. Baskets, pockets, hats, and stockings bulged with fruit; shirt-fronts swelled with it. Dark naked children—some weeping and mortified, others beaming with merriment—flew up and down through the air on frayed ropes like human cranes, to carry armfuls of fruit from the top of the tree to the ground. An elderly woman was trying to haul a large perambulator up into the lime tree with her; a sailor on the ground struck her feet with a belaying pin. She shrieked each time he hit her, but she never relinquished her grip, or her intention to take the black carriage (pray it was unoccupied!) into the tree's highest regions.

Meanwhile, on the ground near her, an amputee had cheerfully removed his wooden leg, and was stuffing it with fruit.

"We have rights! We have rights here!" one fresh-faced sailor shouted, with a gun in one hand and a grimy piece of paper in the other. A pretty young woman—imagine her just an hour earlier, stitching samplers in her parlor, with well-mannered children at her feet—was draped like a hungry leopard over a tree limb six feet above him; she tried to knock him in the head with her bonnet, which was stuffed full of limes.

On the dock, a phalanx of seamen with oppressed and bewildered faces hurried to fill *Estella*'s hull with crates of cargo. Twenty feet away, an old dog was huddled beneath the protective limbs of an old gumbo-limbo tree. He looked afraid of being snatched up and turned into someone's after-dinner pie.

This, then, was *Estella*'s cargo, as coveted and profitable as any other on the world's shipping lanes.

Not sugar. Not tobacco. Not opium.

But *limes*.

And not just any limes, but the smallest and sweetest of the fruit. *Spanish* limes. As dear to the palate as dubloons to the pocket, or emeralds to the breast of a noblewoman.

Nations have gone to war over this diminutive fruit, which, when tossed into the mouth, is said to deliver an instant, drug-like sweetness. Any neighborhood cursed with such a tree is exhorted to grab an ax immediately and chop it down, or be thrown into lawlessness each summer when the fruit reaches perfect ripeness.

We were, I soon learned, a small ship and a small crew. But what we lacked in size we made up for in gumption, traveling the northern islands of Cuba in search of these inestimable limes. Our errand was to transport them to the ports of Florida, where they would be dispersed across the eastern United States.

We eventually weighed anchor, with as many limes as *Estella*'s belly could hold, and set sail from Cayo Dulzura and its riotous inhabitants. A backward glance confirmed that the islanders had now viciously turned one upon the other. The receding pier was a melee of hair-pulling and wrestling, women pushing each other into the sea, men beating each other with palm fronds and rocks.

My final image of the island was of the old woman's perambulator plummeting from the top of the lime tree; it smashed to the ground, spilling fruit in every direction. Fifty or sixty people descended on it, deliriously.

This was, I am sorry to say, my first glimpse of humanity, viewed, as it was, through the tiny air vent of a cargo hold when I was still a small kitten. And although it did not poison my opinion of the entire species, no aspect of it has ever dimmed from my memory. To this day no human face can ever appear in front of me without faintly conjuring up the dark, twisted, lime-greedy faces of the tragically named Cayo Dulzura.

FIVE

or the next six weeks, we sailed forth on water calm as a birdbath. No cross seas or bewitched water ever vexed our bow.

"Could *walk* to Key Largo on water like this," the navigator observed to the mate one morning.

The mate said nothing.

"Ne'er seen a calmer sea than this," the navigator added.

The mate, with grim eyes, was silent.

"Calmest since ninety-three," the navigator remarked.

The mate finally obliged him with a curt nod. He reserved a deep wariness in his heart; you could see it in his face. Like many seasoned sailors, he was suspicious of too much contentment, especially a contented sea. And he disliked talk of contentment even more, as if in bringing the subject into the open made it a conspicuous target, irresistibly alluring to all the darker forces of Fate.

But I am ahead of myself. We did not see our first mast, our first sail, or any other part of the deck or the open sky or the vast world for the first five weeks of our lives. We remained concealed in the bilge with the limes.

The cargo hold was the site of numerous indiscretions, and we became the unseen hosts to a steady stream of visitors morning, noon, and night.

"Do ya have it or not?" a tall man with a silvery beard implored a younger man late one night when most of the rest of the ship was asleep.

The younger man, with a face like a skeleton—except that no skeleton was ever so yellow in color, so scarred from ear to ear, or so agitated in disposition—produced a small parcel from his trousers. "Five dollars," he demanded.

"Four," the man with the beard retorted.

"Five!"

"No more than *four*!"

"Five, you pig!"

"Four, ya stinkin' grampus!"

In an instant, knives flashed, and bloodshed seemed at hand. But whether the man with the beard had appetites that outweighed financial consideration, or the younger man realized a dollar is not worth dying for, I never heard. The deal was struck. The Skeleton fled. Silver Beard sat on a crate. He stuffed a pipe with the black contents of his purchase, and smoked it for a time until, having successfully reduced his eyes to minuscule slivers, he staggered up the steps (slipping once and hitting his head) and out of our presence. His eyes, when he left, were like the glowing red cracks in half-cooled lava.

Another visitor, the ship's cook—a large, benevolent-looking man, a New Englander, with flaming red hair—came down two or three times a week, merely to remove his crumb-flecked shirt and his sauce-stained cap and then dance a little jig, or a waltz. He moved with astonishing agility and verve given the confinement of his surroundings, and an invisible partner floated with equal grace in his arms. Once I heard him murmur the name "Carlotta" with considerable anguish, and he seemed to be hearing in his mind the bright piercing music and kettle drums of a Havana café or a public mascara. This pantomime lasted ten or fifteen minutes before he replaced his shirt and his cap, and returned to deck with a defiant expression, as if hoping—through an intense demeanor—to deflect any suspicion of his secret and rather lovelorn behavior belowdecks.

It was this same cargo hold to which the men came to write letters to their sweethearts; to devour precious foodstuffs they did not want to share with others; to read books in peace (the navigator, a pale, athletic Bostonian, was often here with a candle and a thick volume); and sometimes even to weep unobserved.

But the most unusual of all was the ship's oiler, a slim, swarthy man with black whiskers the size of sausages. He secreted himself in the hold in the darkest hours of the night, when everyone except the Middle Watch was asleep. Then, setting his candle down on a cargo pallet, he proceeded to disrobe entirely, neatly folding his filthy shirt and his filthy breeches. He kept a special box hidden among the crates and opened it with almost trembling fingers. From this large, mysterious container he withdrew the most extraordinary gown: white and yellow silk, with an elaborate brocade of pearls, and a lace and embroidery bodice. A large paper fan, covered with Oriental symbols, was among the accessories. He then donned the gown, squirming and wiggling with enormous effort to pull the bodice over his thick-boned hips, flung open the fan, and proceeded to transform himself, in every gesture and expression, into a dainty lady at court. The fan fluttered flirtatiously in front of his face. He bowed to imaginary admirers.

I even saw him blush, as if he had suffered an indecent proposal. Though the space between the crates was limited, he managed a whirl or two, a curtsey then, and finally a magnificent laugh, as if he had just been complimented on his breathtaking attire. Rarely did he linger in his performance. It seemed enough for him to enjoy a few happy moments in the thrall of this startling transformation. Almost as quickly as he had wiggled into the gown, he wiggled out of it. The majestic silk dress and its paper fan were hurriedly replaced in the box, the box was hidden again, the baggy breeches were soon back on their owner, and he was gone, quickly, like a sprite.

To all of these visitors, we kept our presence strictly concealed until, a month and a half into our travels, our mother introduced us to the real world.

Six

*H*en overboard!" came the cry one morning as my siblings and I dozed on deck. "Man the yawl! Hen overboard!"

There was a scurry of heavy feet. Boot heels barely missed our tails. Orders were barked, countermanded, and counter-countermanded. All was in a tumult.

"Man the yawl!" came the urgent cry again.

The cook emerged from his galley with a look of curiosity, which turned to despair. He ran to the railing with such force I thought he would topple and plunge into the sea. His hands, hair, his face were covered with flour, spice, and gravy—the layers on his trousers were so thick that, by excavating them, one might have discerned the *Estella*'s bill of fare during much of its seagoing career—and he ground his right fist into the palm of his left hand as if one were a mortar and the other a pestle. He scanned the blue water with panic-stricken eyes.

The object of all this distress was the *Estella's* pet chicken, a Cuban red hen named Señorita.

The cook adored this impetuous fowl, and had sworn never to slaughter and roast her, even if, by God, he found himself ship-wrecked on a desert island and she were his only hope of suste-nance; even if the *entire crew* found themselves on the same island and demanded, one and all, that he bake, roast, fricassee, or otherwise prepare her for a final desperate supper. He had raised her from an egg acquired in Havana. Despite her tropical origins, there was nothing unusual about her: she was a chicken, plain and simple. Judging from the cook's protectiveness, it was not absurd to imagine he had sat on the egg himself, night and day, for each of the days necessary to hatch her.

Her feathers in the sunlight were deep brushstrokes of rust and auburn. When the red-headed cook carried the red-feathered fowl on his shoulder, it was difficult to tell from behind where the plumage of the one began and the hackle of the other ended. Per-haps this mutuality of color explained their kinship. Even more intriguing was the sight of the cook asleep on deck, beneath the southern stars, with Señorita curled up against his stomach or in the crook of his arm, her long skinny neck flattened over one or the other of his limbs as if contentedly awaiting the ax.

She had the run of the boat, was accorded more latitude and privilege than anyone aboard. No rules of conduct constricted her leisure; no work schedule plagued her happy hours. More often than not, she was serenely squatted in the middle of the well deck, oblivious and immovable in the sun—except for her tiny, nervous, yellow eyes—while the men sweated, raised sails to the wind, and dashed to accomplish their business around her.

Such was the untroubled state of her life when cries of "Hen overboard!" filled the air.

She had imprudently flown overboard, and now floated and bobbed like a tiny tugboat, some thirty or forty feet off portside. Although her initial flight into the water may have seemed to her like a good idea at the time, she had obviously repented of its wisdom. She clucked and fluttered her wings in horror and dismay as her former home slid farther and farther away from her.

The yawl was lowered. "Get her, boys!" shouted the mate.

Three men, including Silver Beard and the oiler, were recruited to go after her. I'm sorry to add that Silver Beard was in one of those states where his eyes were little more than narrow red fissures: He fell over in the boat three times, seemed oblivious to everything around him, and stood up once as if, having mistaken the yawl for his berth, he were attempting to climb out of it. The yawl looked little bigger than a bathtub, and tottered back and forth in the wildest oscillations, threatening to catapult its occupants into the drink.

The cook shouted near-hysterical encouragements from the railing: "To the left!" "Don't scare her, dammit! Don't scare her!" "No, to the right, God damn you all, to the *right!*" He was obviously prepared, if necessary, to strip and dive into the Straits himself to save her.

A shark was spotted. Or perhaps it was only imagined. The agitation of everyone was increased. I myself had gazed upon this hen with a little knot of hunger in my stomach now and then, and could only guess at the pleasure of a shark presented with such an unexpected and easily acquired appetizer.

But there was not much to worry about. The sea was relatively calm, the *Estella* was traveling no more than four or five knots, and the bird's rescue was smoothly accomplished. The oiler snatched her from the waves; she gave no resistance. He handed her over to Silver Beard, who clutched her to his chest with a look of cross-eyed amazement; she began pecking in his ear as if she had discovered tasty grubs nesting within it.

The cook, near tears, took Señorita in his arms when she was safely on board, and hurried belowdecks with her, all the while muttering terrible recriminations: "*Bad* chicken. Do you know that? Do you know how bad you are? Oh, Señorita, why do you *do* this to me?! Dear Lord, what have I done to deserve this chicken?!" The slamming of the galley door guaranteed that no further adventures would be had with the mischievous fowl that day. And the serving of a meaty chicken broth that night at mess—prepared under Señorita's eyes, from one of her less fortunate brethren—seemed to one and all like a none-too-veiled, though completely idle warning to her.

SEVEN

They groaned, they stirred, they all uprose,
Nor spake, nor moved their eyes;
It had been strange, even in a dream,
To have seen those dead men rise.

—Coleridge, *The Rime of the Ancient Mariner*

*Y*ou did not think that cats read, then? You no doubt presumed we have no literary interests, simply because you have never seen us pull a volume of Proust or Kipling from a bookshelf and read it. But I know many cats who spend more time with—or *in*—the morning newspaper than humans do. And the fact you have never witnessed a phenomenon is no basis for disputing its occurrence. One would be hard-pressed, for example, to prove that birds make love—they consummate their relationships in such privacy. That is how a cat feels about a book.

You will never see cats read, any more than you will catch a raven or a flamingo in the act of *le sport*. I do not mean to be vulgar. Reading is to us a deeply personal experience.

I am preoccupied by the subject of books tonight for two reasons. First, it is a night for books. There are nights for prowling in the hibiscus, nights for love, and nights for tunneling under the bedcovers and sitting, silently, beneath a heavy blanket. Tonight, with its reckless wind and the disquieting chafe of palm fronds against the tin roof overhead, is a night for books, to escape into another, more comforting world. Second, I have recently been looking at a volume of superstitions of the sea—specifically, those superstitions regarding cats.

Estella's first mate took an immense and seemingly insurmountable dislike to us. I do not know why.

Once, many years later, I eavesdropped on a very beautiful countess from Fort-de-France as she ridiculed all cats as grotesquely sexual creatures—shallow, conniving, and self-centered— who gave her the jitters and should therefore be destroyed. But since the very same description could have been applied, with equanimity, to the beautiful countess herself, perhaps it was only yet another case of it takes one to hate one. For two thousand years, we have been maligned, tortured, even burned at the stake.

We have, as a species, been accused of witchery, sensuality, shiftlessness, cold-heartedness, murder, promiscuity, devil worship, even infanticide. There was, in the eighteenth century, a case of a cat having been publicly hanged for allegedly causing, by its mere presence aboard ship, the sinking of a Dutch merchant vessel, the *Count Floris V*, and the loss of half the men onboard. Likewise, in ancient Breton, it was mandatory to kill any tomcat before it reached the age of seven, for fear it would otherwise certainly murder its master. I have no explanation for any of this. Perhaps we are only the mirrors by which men denounce and seek to annihilate the most animalistic aspects of themselves. For man is the only animal on the planet trying to convince himself he is *not* an animal. And what could be more absurd, or more dangerous?

When *Estella*'s cook tried to lure us, four wild kittens, into his confidence with scraps from a watery bouillabaisse that the crew themselves had complained about, so thin and meager was its consistency, the mate marched forward with footsteps like drumfire and towered, disapprovingly, over the situation with his hands on his hips. "If ya love the damned cats so much," he barked with a strange kind of passion, "maybe ya should sleep in the hold with 'em!" He then snatched the paltry leftovers from the fingers of the astonished cook. "Don't encourage 'em," the mate snarled. "I'm warnin' ya for the good of the ship—don't encourage 'em." And he flung the scraps into the sea.

A lanyard on the foremast snapped. We were blamed. Dry rot was discovered. We were blamed. A sudden gale blew from the north, bringing with it spindrifts and high waves. We were blamed for that, as well.

The mate's fanaticism made him seem less like a disgruntled or superstitious seaman and more like a lover scorned, so intense and murderous were his black, shallow eyes. "What have I done," he seethed, "that such miserable creatures should come onto my ship?"

He caught one of my sisters snooping in his cabin and trapped her in a canvas bag, which he was prepared to toss overboard. The bag shook and bounced as he carried it on deck, with the prospect (no doubt) of savoring her slow, cruel suffocation in the water. Her pitiful shrieks and cries were audible through the cloth. But in this case, superstition worked *for* us. To throw a cat overboard would certainly raise a storm—this is the common wisdom of the sea. Every sailor is afraid of retribution for sinking a cat, or any other creature, in the middle of the water. Calmer heads prevailed, the cook and the navigator among them, and my sister was spared. But you could see by the curl of the mate's lips that he would have preferred to drown her, to drown us all.

The Sea

*   *   *

Still, what joy for me to be on the ocean. What memory could be more plain in its pleasure than that of sitting on *Estella's* deck with my mother and siblings close to me, as the great ship dove and rose with the terrain of the sea, first plunging into the waves as if on course for some underwater kingdom, then lifting her bow and taking aim at the sun and the sky. With the wind in my whiskers and the rush of the sea in my ears, I felt I was sailing forth to meet a golden destiny. When you are aboard a ship on a vigorous course with a clear sky ahead, there is always the illusion that every experience waiting for you is a magical one.

You would think that on open water there was only one color, blue, and everything a numbing repetition upon it. But this was never the case. Nothing is less monotonous to the eyes than the sea, and what sea is more prodigiously colored than the Caribbean and its surrounding waters? It is as if the rest of the world had been created first, and there being a surplus of extravagant colors—greens from Brazilian rain forests, reds from the deserts of India, browns and ochers from Africa, gold from the Orient— they were hastily poured into this one place during the final moments of Creation. Colors in the sky, in the water, in the skins of tropical fruit, in fabrics and furnishings brought onboard, in the creatures of the sea and the birds overhead—it often burned the eyes to wrestle with such daily assaults of color and light.

As proof of the peculiar beauty of the region, I offer this anecdote: One night, toward the beginning of the First Watch, after it had been raining for hours, the clouds parted to the east and a full moon suddenly emerged from the darkness. A rainbow formed off the stern of the ship, bold with every conceivable color in the moonlight. It hovered above the dark sea for several minutes, until the moon vanished again behind the clouds. The sight seduced everyone, except for the mate. "No luck in something like that," he hissed under his breath, and then looked down at me as if he might kick me across the deck and over the railing in frustration.

The next day, the mate seemed unduly preoccupied with the wake of the boat—"the following sea"—and was unable to keep his eyes from glancing astern at every opportunity.

"What's *he* fretting about?" a voice behind me asked. It was the Skeleton; he stood, shoulder to shoulder, with Silver Beard. They breathed down my neck with a strong, sickening odor of rum, tobacco, and last night's stew.

"He's been lookin' astern all morning," the Skeleton added.

Silver Beard chuckled, in a grisly, knowing way. "He's watchin' for The Cripple," he said.

The Skeleton snorted and grunted in a great show of knowing exactly who, and what, The Cripple was; but Silver Beard, far more experienced in all manner of lies (even wordless ones), knew in an instant that the Skeleton was shamming.

"The Cripple," explained Silver Beard, as if addressing a simpleton child, "is a lame old duffer with a crutch who appears in the foamy wake of ships doomed to wreck."

The Skeleton looked more skeletal than ever at this grim communication; his normally yellowish cast turned ashen, the color of boiled bones. He seemed tempted to dismiss the story as a mere prank to taunt his immaturity, but instead snorted and grunted, just as he had before. "I *knew* that," he groused, though clearly he had not.

"I was on a ship run down once in a fog on the North Sea," Silver Beard continued, "and the day before it happened three men at the wheel box swore to have seen The Cripple following our boat, limpin' along in her wake as if tryin' to catch up with us and capsize the vessel with his crutch." He paused. "Sixty men were lost," he added.

The Skeleton trembled. He coughed. It took him a moment to

regain his voice. "So," he said, "why's *he* looking for The Cripple anyway? Is he thinkin' we'll wreck?"

Silver Beard didn't reply at once, but leveled his intense eyes across the deck. "He's sure to have his reasons," he muttered darkly—and I suddenly realized they had shifted their gaze to me.

EIGHT

$\mathcal{T}$ hen at La Esperanza, on the northwest Cuban coast, we took on fresh cargo—limes, limes, the bilge brimming with limes. *Estella*'s dark belly settled comfortably in the water as a wealthy man sated from supper settles deep into his easy chair. The cook acquired a small snake there. Dockhands had captured and restrained the creature with the sole intention of torturing it for their amusement, as I have no doubt they also tortured birds, insects, scorpions, and any other creature unfortunate enough to pass before their bored and restless eyes on those lonely docks.

The condemned serpent lay coiled and motionless in a small wire basket, inadequately shaded by giant ragged banana trees—

themselves neglected and persecuted by lack of rain—at one end of the wharf. It had been starved for a week in anticipation of its eventually putting up an even more entertaining struggle for the men when they got to it.

Appalled, the cook offered a bottle of brandy in exchange for it. The proposition aroused incredulity among the crew and laughter from the Portuguese dockhands. The dockhands sensed even more profit to be wrenched from the cook's kind heart, and demanded *two* bottles of brandy, which—to renewed laughter—the cook handed over. Two bottles of brandy! Aboard most vessels, two bottles of brandy was the considerable penalty for cheating at cards. Two bottles of brandy in any port could purchase a pair of healthy mules, several pairs of new boots, or even—on many islands—a bride.

The snake itself was not much of a snake. It was difficult to imagine what sport could be had tormenting such an innocuous thing. It was no more than eighteen inches long, with brilliant bands of yellow, crimson, and black along its entire length; it was scarcely larger than the vein in a man's bicep. Its relaxed and dulcet eyes, mildly examining the world, betrayed anything *but* a sinister nature. Like most of us, it wanted only to be left alone.

When the cook tried to take the creature onto *Estella*, the mate stood in his way. "You're not bringing that onboard," the mate announced with emphatic annoyance.

"I'll take anything onboard I like," countered the cook, with equal intensity.

"A snake's bad luck," said the mate.

"To hell with your luck," muttered the cook.

"To hell with your snake," grumbled the mate.

A loud and unhappy discourse followed. It looked as if the mate and the cook would scuffle on the gangway; but the cook finally won the argument by threatening to give salted squid—the dreaded "salt slug"—to the crew for a month. "I know your love of creatures," snarled the mate as the cook marched past him. "I know ya think you're better'n all of us because of it."

The cook said nothing.

" 'Twas a snake that forced Adam out of paradise," a crewman near me whispered to another.

" 'Twas a snake that killed Cleopatra," whispered a third. "I read so in a book."

"No good for a snake to be onboard," whispered the first, and he and the other two, scheming in their minds, exchanged meaningful glances.

No good for a snake to be onboard: that was soon the watchword aboard ship, muttered over soup, grumbled on deck, whispered in the berths. A stealthy dissatisfaction that, like a poorly tied knot in a bowline, promised to do bigger things in the near future.

"You're daft as they come, Daniel," the navigator lectured the cook one morning. "Do ya not know what kind of snake that is? A coral snake, man. Most lethal on the globe. Ya shoulda let them kill it on the dock."

The cook stared at the navigator with the same burning cheeks with which he'd confronted the mate.

"A snake has no feelings," the navigator continued. "It would never have known what was happening to it when those dockhands had their fun with it."

"It's convenient to think so," replied the cook, with barely restrained passion.

"*I* wasn't going to torment it," the navigator griped defensively. "I only say the creature itself would never have known the difference."

"Why do you suppose a snake feels nothing, when you feel every injustice against *you?*" asked the cook, his lips trembling with anger.

"Argue with God," snapped the navigator. "It's God's plan that men have souls and creatures do not."

"It's *vanity* that makes men think so," replied the cook.

From that moment on, the snake was always with the cook. It

coiled around his neck like a necklace of bright beads as he cut onions and peppers in preparation for the evening mess; it swam in and out of his collar as he scrubbed the galley floor. Sometimes it hung around his wrist, a living charm bracelet (but not so charming to others), with its head horizontal from the rest of its body and its ever-busy tongue exploring the current state of the sea air. It even slept with the cook and Señorita. This odd marriage disturbed the crew entirely, since they saw bleak auguries in the forced co-existence of hen and serpent, though not a man aboard could pinpoint or explain the unsettling quality of it. I myself thought it a strange and wonderful scene—the cook, like a human Ark, with his animals aboard him having found salvation. I cannot find the proper words, but from a cat's point of view the division is always clear: There are people who destroy, and people who mend and enrich. Nature, in the form of its innocent creatures, flocks to those who mend things.

Predictably, the snake disappeared two weeks after it came aboard. No one ever confessed, and no accusations were ever leveled, but it was presumed by all that the insignificant creature had perished among its primeval ancestors in the sea, having been tossed into the black waves one night by an unhappy shipmate.

In retaliation, the cook gave the crew "salt slug" for a week, and never again had affable words for any man onboard.

NINE

$\mathcal{B}$ut the worst of it came barely seven days later, in the waning days of October—always an unlucky month—when having dispatched one load of limes north to the Florida coast, *Estella* returned south to La Esperanza for another. The weather, like an adolescent boy suddenly ashamed of too much passivity or gentleness, turned heavy and foul and gave a great exhibition of muscle. Squalls whipped the vessel, and there was intense rain, cold for the time of year, as if it had blown south from Newfoundland or Baffin Bay. It was possible to be sailing beneath a clear azure sky one moment, then enter a black convulsion that pitched the boat without mercy for an hour. "Blowing great guns and small arms," said the navigator. Dark waterspouts attended the squalls, and

danced above the surface of the sea all around us. Just as abruptly, we would sail back into sunshine again.

The sea, as a rule, ran high and rough, though *Estella*—with favorable, if sometimes unpredictable winds—managed nine knots.

It was at this fateful time that Señorita decided to go for a swim.

She fled the galley one morning, and fluttered onto the deck in the middle of a fierce rainstorm. Whether the rain and high sea confused her, or merely invited her to seek more clement conditions elsewhere, she hopped onto the railing to survey the ocean and, after a series of annoyed squawks, plummeted over the starboard side of the vessel and onto the menacing sea.

"Hen overboard!" came the frantic cry. "Man the yawl! Hen overboard!"

Boots marched. Voices hollered. The yawl was untied. Despite the brutality of the rain, there was an odd festivity and enthusiasm on deck.

"Hen overboard!"

Here, if nothing else, was an opportunity to mend strained feelings and relationships, to pull together for a common cause and cast aside the dark resentments that had been brewing on ship for a week.

But the captain put a quick stop to it.

The seas were thick and lofty, the wind formidable; we were

moving at a fast clip. The rain poured down, but more alarmingly the waves seemed to rain *up*: thick misty veils flew off the ocean surface and spun, in miniature cyclones, skyward. In such weather, the captain refused to risk any crewman to save the bird.

The cook pleaded with the captain. So did the oiler and the mate. But the captain rebuffed them all. He would not lose any man for the sake of a chicken.

By then it was nearly impossible to see poor Señorita on the water, so dense were the streams of rain, ocean, and wind whirling around her. One heard an occasional sad cluck, or a mystified squawk as she drifted away from us. Was she sensible of the horror attending her irretrievable situation? Not a movement, not a voice, could be heard on deck, so still and silent was every man, straining ears for Señorita's voice on the open sea, until at last we lost all connection with her, castaway forever as she was in the middle of a pitiless ocean.

A deep gloom and silence settled upon the vessel afterward. The cook sat in his galley. He came out only once, an hour after Señorita's disappearance, and cast his eyes over the sea, now maddeningly calm and turquoise blue. "Señorita!" he suddenly howled. "Señorita!" until the men dragged him below and gave him rum to make him oblivious.

After that morning, the mate's intensity of superstition deep-

ened; no mouth was ever so clenched, so full of apprehension. Silver Beard retreated deeper into his opium dreams; and once, when the Skeleton tried to make a callow jest about the vanished bird, Silver Beard laid him flat on his back with one swift whack of the hand.

I think we all of us knew then, in our hearts, that the *Estella* was doomed.

TEN

$\mathcal{T}$he storm that finally ended *Estella*'s career began as a small black cloud racing toward the ship from the southeast. The mate watched it come on us, as if it were the scouting party for a belligerent army.

"Dirty weather, sir?" asked the oiler.

"More than that," muttered the mate, with odd resignation.

There was no wind. The sea was eerily calm. The heat was suffocating, intolerable, and carried an awful smell within it, like metal filings, as if a distant blacksmith were at work filing the earth to dust.

The distant reaches of the eastern sky were cobalt blue, gray, and black. The sight called to mind ancient maps marking the end of the known world with a grim thick line and the bleak warning: "There be dragons here."

The ship began to roll—a peculiar thing, since the ocean itself was waveless and flat. Sitting on deck under the lifeless afternoon sun, I watched a stray mast-bolt, little bigger than my head, totter one way, then the other, then back again; it described a small circle with its pendulous path, but waltzed no more than two or three inches in either direction. The sunlight began to acquire a distinctly pink coloration. Not pretty. Deathly. The most ugly and oppressive shade of pink I've ever seen.

The ominous rolling increased, so incongruous with a quiet sea that as yet revealed no trace of its future plans. The mast-bolt was soon rolling nearly a foot either way in front of me. The foremast overhead sighed with anxiety. The mainmast replied with its own misgivings. I'd never felt air so close—you felt as if you'd been entombed in it.

"Barometer's still tumbling," said the navigator.

"I know," said the mate grimly, staring into the ever-darkening cavern ahead of us.

Preparations for the storm began methodically: not slowly, but decisively, with an artificial lack of alarm, as if the crew convinced themselves that nothing exceptional would happen if only they themselves acted in no exceptional way. There was little conversation. None of the usual chaffing. A stronger-than-usual breeze fluttered through the sails, then died back to a dead calm. The air began to smell of rain. Lightning dotted the horizon: blinding, wide, stumplike bolts that lingered a moment too long between sky and sea.

As a precaution against the coming tumult that now filled nearly half the eastern sky, my mother led us below to the cargo hold. The last I saw of the day was the sun swallowed by legions of ravenous clouds. It did not look like a storm coming; it looked like the arrival of God. At the same instant the waves surrounding the ship began to boil. An endless riot of silver fish— thousands of them—vaulted out of the sea; tarpon, snook, mullet, even barracuda, eels, and rays, all fleeing in advance of the black clouds.

The strong winds rose all at once.

With one sudden burst, like an angry hand trying to shove us away, the ship nearly heeled. It righted itself, to be badgered and bullied again. And again.

The spinning and convulsing that attended my birth were only rehearsals for the wild maelstrom we were instantly engulfed in. The ship no longer rolled; it thrashed. The wind did not blow; it screamed—an endless deafening roar punctuated by ear-piercing whistles. The bow seemed to go in one direction, the stern in another, then the stern concurred with the bow, but not before the bow had changed its mind, and they were pulling in opposite directions again.

Riggings and spars were carried away before anyone knew they were gone.

The sound in the shrouds began like that of something tearing.

The shouts from the deck were all at once for mercy, for help, for sanctuary. The tattered sails took flight, upward, like panicked birds. *Estella* seemed to lift off the waves, as if suspended in the middle of the angry wind.

The timbers in the hold contracted and expanded, then cracked and popped as if battered from outside with an immense ram. Water squirted in, like white, watery hands slipping between the seams of the ship and reaching for us. Limes, limes, everywhere limes, and broken crates and flying wood, and everything doused with sheets of water. We went up, we went down, the hull hit the water with a force that made it seem certain the sea had turned to granite. And the wind: Even in the hold you could feel its pressure, hear its screech. It does not take long for a ship to break apart in a hurricane. When you imagine it, safely at home, you think, I would have time to save myself; only fools and cowards lose their heads.

Nothing could be further from reality.

Timbers exploded, and the bilge began to flood. The jibboom vanished. The ship had no masts, only stumps; no deck, only scraps and shards and slivers. It was like being in the middle of a crumbling tower of cards, the destruction of *Estella* was so quick, so effortless a feat. Crockery heaved against a stone floor shatters less thoroughly. The gale winds and the rain worried her to death from above, the reefs chewed her up from below.

All at once we were in the open water, pelted by rain as heavy and hard as buckshot. My siblings and I clutched a heaving crate of limes with such terror that our claws were scarcely less tenacious than iron nails. There was no sign of our mother. Casks, planks, and bulwarks tumbled over us. I saw a huge iron pot still full of soup, by God, with bits of meat bobbing in it, twirl by on the waves. I saw a bookcase dance on the sea, held upright by the wind; its charts, documents, and volumes were pressed into their usual place by the force of the gale.

The oiler's yellow gown rushed past us, like a giant jellyfish trapped in a racing, whirling current. The snake—not tossed overboard after all, but having hidden itself away in some dim part of the vessel—blew by us next, poor creature, struggling on the waves and trying to wrap itself, futilely, around a piece of what had once been the quartermast.

Silver Beard drowned near me. It happened so quickly it

seemed impossible to have happened at all. His red, horrified eyes were the last thing I ever saw of him. Swept away, all swept away, everything that had been *Estella* and her crew.

I saw the cook riding away on what looked like a bed, his eyes wide with terror and disbelief. Like a bizarre lifeboat, the bed went up and down with the waves, a stray sheet fluttering madly in the wind. He sailed away into a cruel black mist before I lost all sight of him.

The sea was full of limes, swarming like insects. Limes churning, bobbing, crashing into one another. The head of the navigator suddenly appeared near us, erupting through a surface of limes. He gasped. He clawed at the limes as if expecting them to buoy him. He was carried off by a sudden wave so full of limes his head became indistinguishable from the fruit.

The silence of the men as they drowned was cruel. Better to have heard them shrieking and pleading in the water. The overwhelming clamor of the storm filled my ears: the rain, the wind, the surf. But the men—they went to their fates in eerie muteness. There were none of the sobs and screams that accompany a wreck in fiction and fancy. Not a one. Only a dark, speechless submission to the fury of the ocean and the wind.

Our crate began to twirl and flounder. The force of its convulsions heaved us into the water. I felt—nothing. One is supposed to feel a profound revelation at the moment of death. Death is the great cataclysm: accompanied by every emotion one has experienced in life, a magnifying glass that focuses all the sensations of existence into a single searing point. But I felt nothing. Having had so little experience of life, I had little reaction to its approaching conclusion.

We continued spinning, though the crate was now gone from beneath us. Water filled my ears, my mouth, and my eyes. My siblings and I crashed uncontrollably into one another. We tried to paddle with our paws to stay afloat. And then I knew: Death was at hand. We were, I am certain, less than an instant from its clutch—when all at once a cabin door whirled into us and the four of us, miraculously, clawed our way aboard it.

Suddenly I felt a human hand come up from behind me, as if to drag me back into the seething water. I turned and saw, through the foam and the blinding rain, the mate. His face was dark, wet, bleeding, and angry, an anger so deep and potent it could no longer express itself with simple profanities or retribution. An anger that transforms the body and the soul. He grabbed for me again, but failed. He tried to seize the entire door, but a wave knocked him back, away from us. "Ya cursed the ship the moment you were born!" he screamed into the wind. "Now ya can live with it the rest of your days!"

The Sea

I suddenly realized he had my mother in one arm; she was crushed between his forearm and his chest, and was struggling to fight free of him with what little energy she had left. But he held her in a death grip, intent on taking her down to the ocean floor with him. Her wet face, her wet fur, her terrified eyes—these were my final glimpses of her.

And then, she and the mate were gone. Gone. Consumed by the storm. I saw them last, only for a moment, as the mate tried to outmaneuver a frenzied herd of mammoth waves that descended on him from every direction. But there was no escape route. He and my mother were devoured by them.

Any relief I may have felt at our salvation was short-lived. No reprieve from the hurricane awaited us. I turned and saw an army of enormous rocks race toward us. Black, glistening rocks lashed by the wind and the sea. It took a moment to realize they were not coming at us—we were hurtling toward them. The speed of the approach snatched the breath from my lungs. My heart froze. We would be crushed. A black wave lifted us up one last time, seemed to hold us in the gale for a longer than expected moment as if to savor our pain and terror, and then dropped us onto the rocks with such force that the door beneath us shattered into a thousand splinters.

Down, down, down into the sea, among fish and sea worms

and crabs. Seaweed coiled around my limbs and pulled me deeper into the awaiting blackness. What strange narcotic, the hush of the underwaters. Not even the accidental brush of a lifeless human hand—to whom it belonged I will never know—could arouse me from a deepening torpitude and indifference.

Enchanted Ground

Enchanted Ground

ELEVEN

*G*od, give me peace from the rain. It is falling now as I write this memoir. It wants to come in around the seams of my window; it hisses against the eaves. The wind, its accomplice in all things terrible, is so rampant—and from the northeast!—that every door is chattering in its frame like the teeth of an old sailor on a foggy First Watch. If there is a plank loose anywhere on the house tonight, it is complaining, loudly. "Let me in, let me in," the storm seems to wail. But the infirmities of old age run so deep I often hear voices where none exist.

For several days I have watched the progress of a dark-red wasp, so narrow and delicate it's difficult to comprehend how all the necessary organs of life are contained within it. It is building a paper nest in a corner of my window, protected by the overhang of the blue hurricane shutters. Tonight, there are suddenly two wasps. They are very still, as if they had winter in their blood. I myself could imagine it is cold outside, that instead of travelers' palms and brilliant orchids there are leafless lilacs and hibernating elms. It is that kind of night: when the seasons of the heart take precedence over the seasons of the calendar.

The lighthouse is almost directly outside my window. There are nights when I look to the top and can see myself there, a silhouette against the moonlight: strong, and brave, and full of myself. Young still. Young once. But not tonight. Too much rain, too much wind. The storm gathers strength, the mist thickens, just as time itself draws an increasingly thick curtain between us and our memories.

TWELVE

We owed our deliverance from danger then, the four of us, castaways of *Estella*, to an eccentric child with a heart as deep and enigmatic as the sea.

The edge of the terrible hurricane had moved on to other shores and other ships at sea, and left no trace of its visit in the sky. The shoreline, on the other hand, bore bleak testimony to the storm and the wreck of our vessel. Planks and pots and rope, and oh, so many limes. Part of a topgallant lay snapped over the rocks, and an open, upside-down trunk sat halfway on shore and halfway in the water, as if uncertain to which world it now belonged. Books and candlesticks, and even a trio of plump Dutch cheeses bound in burlap had been washed ashore. A broad piece of *Estella*'s mainsail was draped, sopping, over an immense rock; Fate, with a keen sense of humor, had given this rock the un-expected appearance of an enormous upholstered chair. Except that no chair was ever so visited with blue crabs and perplexed dragonflies.

Of *Estella*'s crew there was no trace.

The child came lumbering over the rocks toward us, and ap-peared to be chatting happily with no one but himself. His face was at first indistinguishable from the blinding just-risen sun. A girl's voice called in the distance: "Griffin! Oh, Grif-*fin!*" as if it were the duty of every sister to disrupt the secret explorations of a younger brother.

The boy's hands were full of salvaged shipwreck debris, and there was to his salvaging an air of happy indecision, as if the shore were not scattered with wreckage but bewildering Christ-mas presents, all to be gained for the taking. Fine brass glinted be-tween his fingers. A silver ladle was plunged down the front of his shirt. As he drew closer, I realized he was not talking to himself at all. He was conversing with the face of a clock—a charming brass clock I recognized as having once hung on the wall of the cap-tain's cabin.

"It's all right," he reassured the clock. "I'll give you a good home now. Don't be afraid. You'll come home with me." The clock, whatever its gratitude, did not respond at once, not even with a rattle or a click, having been badgered into silence by its unexpected and traumatic arrival ashore.

Pockets full of treasures: One did not need to see them, one could hear them—clank, clank, *clink*—with every step. Bolts and spoons and brass hinges filled the boy's trousers, weighed him down with bulges on either side of his hips, like too much ballast.

"Griffin! Where *arrrrrre* you? Mama wants you."

When at last he came upon us, amid the splinters of the cabin door that had been our final conveyance through the storm, the clanking in his pockets abruptly stopped.

A giant crab hovered on the rocks above us, its strange eyes like tiny black seeds in a liquidy seed pod. It was waiting to see what action the boy would take—and was trying to decide whether kittens, a delicacy previously unknown on these rocky shores, would make a satisfactory breakfast after all.

The boy's small fingers went to his lips. His black eyes grew wide. He set down the clock, but gently, as if mindful of its injuries. He whispered something inaudible to himself, and then bent down and tentatively touched the very tip of his index finger to the very tip of my left ear. My ear fluttered, entirely of its own accord. He then gathered the four of us to his chest—to the apparent disappointment of the crab, which made a quick series of annoyed steps backward—and carried us back to the light-house, along the treacherous overhangs the hurricane had carved from the shore overnight.

"Griffin! *Come on!* What have you got there? Oh, let me see. Oh, Mama's gonna be *mad* when she sees this. . . ."

The look on his mother's face when he came into the house with an armful of half-drowned kittens—well, his mother, Mary, was a realist. I suspect she was not pleased by Griffin's most recent discovery. But Griffin, like all good people, had already achieved a passionate protectiveness toward us, the defiance of childhood in pursuit of a noble cause: "If you make me take them back to the beach, Mama, you must make me go live at the beach, too."

Anyone who has ever rescued an injured dog or a stray kitten will applaud such fierceness immediately, I am sure.

THIRTEEN

*B*ut where are we, then? To what place had the hurricane, in its awful indifference, delivered us?

This remote and unearthly island—it is neither here nor there.

It is not Caribbean, but neither is it wholeheartedly American, despite the Stars and Stripes that billow (many would say, without welcome) above its customs house.

It is not the jungle, but few would call it civilization, so scant, so rough, so *un*civilized are its amenities, so completely removed is it from the stir of all glamorous society.

It is weather-beaten, flat, and craggy. Despite the heat and profusion of tropical blooms, it has more in common with the English moors than nearby Cuba, though the desolate moors are more than five thousand miles away and pretty Havana, with its fertile fields, gay volantes, and noisy *bulevares*, is less than a hundred.

Prim white houses, hallmarks of prosperity and taste, rise from the bed of unyielding white coral that passes here for earth. Giant coconut palms, like aging majordomos, stand guard around the windows; they sway in the endless breezes that blow first from the Atlantic and then, contradicting themselves, from the Gulf of Mexico. An excessive slant permanently disfigures the trees: They are forever seeking charity from the breeze. And they are, during the dry season, as white as the houses, so much coral dust adheres to them. But there are also tin hovels here, low metal shanties that are rusty and very noisy when the wind comes up (for nothing makes a racket like tin in a gale)—examples of shocking poverty. The hovels are all the more conspicuous for *their* lack of trees or other protection from the sun.

Only one degree of latitude separates these islands from the Tropic of Cancer, and they bake beneath a pitiless sky. The natural flora is meager, and grows low to the ground. Sea grape, poisonwood, mangrove—it dares not assert itself more vigorously, lest it be scorched. And if some wayward branch reaches higher than the others, no matter—a hurricane will come along every five or six years to humble it.

Shade and coolness are the most sought-after commodities, and the division is not so much between rich and poor, upper class and lower class, landowner and laborer, as it is between those who have shade and coolness and those who do not. In Boston, Philadelphia, and New York, prosperity announces itself with furs, jewels, and luxurious carriages; here, the most conspicuous displays of prosperity are shutters, wide terraces, imported palm trees, and servants to wave newspapers in your face.

And yet, this white, dry, hot uncivilized island, peopled by every renegade and escapee from civilization imaginable, this island is surrounded by the most beautiful ocean in the world, a shallow, shifting, translucent sea of improbable blues and greens. There are people who have arrived for a week and never left, the color of the water so thoroughly bewitched them. When they thought of leaving, the sea took over their minds. A tremor of pain passed through their bodies, as if they recalled a wonderful lover, and they could not go. No, could never go, could never return to the real world—or risked weeping in winter up north over the warm azure ocean they had left behind.

The early Castilian explorers called the island Los Martires; they mistook the tortured, twisted shapes of the mangroves for Christian souls in pious torment. Later, the island was dubbed

Cayo Hueso, the Island of Bones, a reference to the shards of coral scattered everywhere, bleached to an ossiferous texture beneath the unsparing sun. Today, it is known simply—to mariner and armchair traveler alike—as Key West.

FOURTEEN

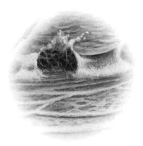

*G*riffin lived with his mother and his older sister, Ada, the three of them alone together in a small white house with Bahama green shutters and a widow's walk. It was no more than thirty feet from the lighthouse, and was separated from that imposing tower by a gentle garden of sapodilla trees and airy philodendrons. His mother was the lighthouse keeper.

It was not unheard of for women to be lighthouse keepers. They were rarely assigned to the post directly, but had to inherit it from a husband or father. Men fell ill, died, or went off to war; who better to take their places than wives and daughters, women who knew how to cajole and flatter the delicate machinery of the light? A lighthouse lens needs more pampering and attention than a mistress. Shouldn't trust it to strangers. The Lighthouse Service was not especially progressive; but pragmatism has often hastened the cause of feminine liberation where other paths to equality took their time.

Mary Bishop was not the first woman to tend the Key West lighthouse. Kathleen Mobriaty was barely nineteen when she inherited the job from her father, who died in the yellow fever epidemic of 1840. His last words to her were "Mind the light." Sadly, she succumbed to the same epidemic herself four weeks later, whereupon the duties and obligations of the lighthouse fell to an even younger sister, who did indeed faithfully "mind the light," through every conceivable weather, for more than thirteen years— until a visiting bosun's mate took her away from both the lighthouse and Key West.

In 1861, Lucy Kneebone assumed the duties of the light after her husband, Edwin, was shot during a game of poker at a waterfront bar on Caroline Street. An attractive, well-proportioned, and flamboyant woman, legendary for her attachment to immense sunbonnets and blinding aniline dyes, she was forcibly relieved of her duties two years later. Not because of her sex, or for want of competence, but because she was discovered to be hiding Confederate spies in the lighthouse tower. The rest of Florida had joined the Confederacy, but Key West—with a mind of its own— had allied with the North.

Women were as suited as men to the physical demands of the light, even when it came to launching dinghies on black and stormy nights to rescue shipwrecked seamen. For their efforts, they received five hundred dollars a year. Scant pay, but better than the workhouse, or living off the unpredictable generosity of relatives, as was the destiny of almost any unallied female in that era.

At the time of which I write, Griffin's father had been dead for eight years, having perished one summer morning while cleaning the gutters that provided water to the family cistern. He climbed onto the roof, lost his footing, tumbled over the edge, and broke his neck.

His wife, Mary, assumed his post then. At least four times a day she could be seen climbing the long, gracefully winding iron staircase to the top of the tower: once to wind the mechanism that kept the light in motion at night (the machinery was like a giant, fairy-tale clock); once to haul up enormous cans of kerosene on a rope from the oil house; once in the evening to remove the impenetrable canvas drapes that protected the delicate Fresnel lens from sunlight; and once again, just after dawn, to put the drapes back into place.

It was eighty-eight steps up, and eighty-eight steps down, each and every time she made the climb.

When not actually tending the lamp, she often sat at the bottom of the spiral staircase and sewed by the light that beamed down through the clockwork weight hole in the deck of the lantern.

*F*IFTEEN

*W*ithin twenty-four hours of our rescue, one of my sisters had died.

I cannot dwell on it even now, except to wonder: Is any sight more challenging to a basic sense of optimism than a lifeless juvenile of any species? These cruel and premature deaths, they reduce Life to a less compassionate stature than the merest mortal, who given such power would spare a young thing the horrors of suffering and death. Not so Life herself: She wields her power with caustic whimsy. For the rest of us, we can wholeheartedly—and for once, unselfishly—put our faith in a beneficent afterlife.

Griffin was not a child to leave important matters in the hands of God. He conscientiously nursed us. He passionately, zealously nursed us. A medicine dropper was used to feed us warm milk and honey. An old robe of his mother's, destined for the rag box, kept us wrapped up and warm. Our fur was kept clean of fleas and filth with an otherwise unemployed doll's hairbrush.

And each time Griffin fed us, he leaned over and whispered into our small ears—with an intensity that belied his age, and seemed to conjure the least tangible laws of Nature—"You are going to live. You're going to *live*." As if he were casting a spell around us.

At night, he curled up on a blanket on the floor, the arc of his torso like a fortress wall around our bodies, as if death might creep in and steal us were he not present to repel its advances. His mother's objections to this sleeping arrangement were futile, and half-hearted anyway, I suppose. She prepared a fire in the parlor, and moved him and us next to it. Mary Bishop—slim, sturdy, severe at first glance, with her tightly wound hair, her plain dress, and her metal-framed eyeglasses—was not one of God's fools. She knew the pricelessness of her son's generous nature.

Her favorite white wicker rocking chair was next to the hearth. Late at night she sat and rocked and studied the scene before her: her son and his shipwrecked charges. Her eyeglasses gleamed with a reflection of the fire. Her attentive eyes appraised the scene as any mother's would, with unmistakable admiration and love; but also wonderment, as if she were asking herself from what mysterious fountainhead this little boy's preternatural passion for life and small creatures sprang. Those closed dark eyes of his, so abnormally large in waking, as if able to see more, and suffer more, moved her. She had rarely encountered any person, let alone a child, so oddly alienated from his own species, but so at ease with every other.

The great mahogany clock on the parlor wall struck a very late hour before she finally went to bed.

She was not alone presiding over her son's ministrations. A large gold dragon filled an entire wall of the parlor, a gift many years earlier from the sailors of a Chinese freighter that was saved from the reef by the lighthouse. Sculpted from wood and gilded with gold leaf, it had eyes and claws that were painted blood-red. It shimmered on the wall at night, seemed to come alive and squirm restlessly in the hot shadows cast by the fireplace. Odd, how sympathetic it seemed to our plight. The sight of it never alarmed me. It gave me queer comfort.

Not so the guests who dashed through the house each day: neighbors, hired help, merchants, and friends. They oohed and aahed over our presence, but demonstrated little sympathy or understanding for the great battle of survival we were engaged in.

"But do you think it's *wise* to have wild kittens in the house?" they asked. "One of the children might catch something." Mary Bishop concealed a laugh—or at least a smile—thinking of a sight not yet twenty-four hours old in her memory: her son's sleeping head nuzzled amid a promiscuous potpourri of paws, furry ears, and striped tails.

Not only were there wild kittens in the house; her son was living among them as if the gulf between species did not exist.

Another two or three days came and went. Another of my sisters died.

Still, Griffin leaned over and whispered in our ears, "You are going to live. *Live . . .*"

It occurred to everyone then, except Griffin, that the litter was doomed. When Griffin had first discovered us, we were badly dehydrated: fleas had already begun to feast on our bodies. Two of us had been weakened beyond repair, beyond even the healing powers of a nine-year-old boy with a huge and relentless heart. I and my brother were all who remained.

My brother struggled valiantly to stay in this world. I could feel his struggle, the passion of his body for life; that so tiny a body had *any* power to defy death was unthinkable. I heard his labored breathing next to me, a rhythm so shallow and erratic it seemed certain to cease at any moment. Still, he clung to life. "You're go-

ing to live," Griffin whispered in his ear. "You're going to liv
The strange incantation was more passionate than ever.

Meanwhile, at the same hour every night, Mary Bisho
up her vigil in the wicker chair, as if it were necessary for
one to watch over the watcher. And every night, there w
same look upon her face. Maternal, certainly. Concerned. B
full of something else, as if in witnessing her son's tug-of-wa
Death, his inability to let Death simply have its way, sh
peering into the innermost mysteries of the human heart.

Later, in the middle of the night, I woke to muffled sob
looked up. Mary Bishop's chair was empty. The fire had di
dull, simmering orange. I feared the worst. Even the
dragon on the wall looked forlorn. My poor brother, I was
was dead.

Griffin's arms were locked around my brother's body. H
head was pressed against my brother's belly. He began t
with God. My brother was still alive. Griffin bargained for
significant life held there in the crook of his arm: "Pleas
kill him. What has he done to you? Let *me* have him, I
good care of him. I'll give them a good life. I promise. Pl
me have them"—a negotiation that every honest read
concede an intimate knowledge of, for who among us has

73

least once in our lives, been awake at three in the morning with a creature we love dying beside us?

Later, I heard it said that I alone of the entire litter seemed capable of survival. I was plumper than the others. I recovered from the shipwreck more quickly. But my brother—oh, it was a sad and precarious week. Griffin would not let go. And my brother could not hold on. I don't think there was a force in the universe that could have convinced Griffin to yield to a higher authority. And then finally, after ten anxious days, my brother made a turn for the better. He overcame the worst. He survived. And yet he was, for always after that, a frail creature, the mark of the shipwreck and the subsequent illness plain to see, as if in letting him survive for a time longer the illness had, in exchange, demanded that it always have one hand on him, a reminder.

And so we became Fafner and Mrs. Moore, the names pulled from who knows what inspiration or private caprice. I never knew. I do not remember any discussion of the matter. Mary Bishop took one look at me one morning and said, without hesitation, "Mrs. Moore." The children laughed, as if at some common joke.

And to this day, though it was more than three decades ago, I can still hear Griffin Bishop's obstinate voice in my ear: "You are going to live. *Live . . .*"

I believe now that it was his will, his passion, that penetrated like a medicine into our cells, and that even now there is inside of me, at the heart of me, some indestructible grains of that soul that was uniquely his.

SIXTEEN

Keepers must be courteous and polite to all visitors and show them everything of interest about the station at such times as will not interfere with light-house duties. . . . No visitors should be admitted to the tower unless attended by a keeper. . . .

—*Instructions to Light-Keepers*, the U.S. Lighthouse Service, 1898

The Reverend Neighbor came to call on us. The Reverend William Neighbor. Late of Palebriar, New Jersey. A resident of the island for three and a half years. I cannot say to which church or denomination he belonged, for cats do not concern themselves with such distinctions. Of what use to *us* are the infinite hair-splittings of people who wish to parse God's miraculous creation as if it were a drab sentence? He was a Reverend—that's all I knew.

He was broad-shouldered and muscular, in his middle to late

thirties, with hair so thick and dark a frigatebird flying overhead might have been forgiven mistaking him for a lost member of the family. His deep brown eyes were probing—they had not yet lost all the pedantry and priggishness of youth—but steadfastly lenient, as if it were his incorruptible nature to look for injustice to correct, bewilderment to ease. He was handsome—oh, yes, handsome in the extreme—with an invigorating, extraordinarily agreeable smell to him. The hem of his trousers smelled faintly of mango weed, as if he had danced lightly through a patch in bloom on his way to the lighthouse.

He was laughing easily and capriciously, though there was nothing especial to laugh at. But I soon learned he laughed a great deal in the presence of Mary Bishop, as if she were a fire and he were a pot of coffee and he could not help warming in her presence.

"New additions to the congregation?" he said as he sat down. Fafner and I sat on the floor, side by side, next to his chair.

"Griffin," was all Mary Bishop replied, with a smile.

"Yes, Griffin," said the Reverend Neighbor in thoughtful agreement. He reached down and scratched my ear. "Your son is . . ." His voice trailed off, as if he could not find the proper adjective, as if the right adjective had not yet been coined. Suddenly he thought of one. "Egalitarian," he suggested.

"Not so egalitarian as you may believe," she responded. "He holds scorpions and lizards in *much* higher regard than any of us."

"Having spent the morning counseling the O'Grady newly-weds"—he shook his head over the sad but obviously deplorable state of the O'Grady union—"I'm not so sure I don't sometimes agree with him."

Mary Bishop looked away.

"Would you take some tea?" she asked, and those usually stern cheeks suddenly glowed with a momentary blush. She was not a pretty woman. There was much of the schoolmarm about her, and what prettiness there was, in the lips for example, she did everything to conceal and repress. She, too, was in her late thirties, but kept her pale brown hair so tightly bound and dressed with such severity—a proper white dress with no ornamentation, such as a missionary's wife might have worn—she could have been construed for ten years older from a distance.

The blush seemed to aggravate her. Of what use was a blush? Like a gossip it only announced to the world what one would rather keep to oneself. She brushed at her cheeks, trying to eliminate it, the way one dispatches an annoying hair dangling down the bridge of one's nose.

He had not asked for the tea, but she handed it to him anyway, and scrupulously avoided any contact between their fingers in the process.

"Actually," the Reverend Neighbor said, "I was hoping you'd escort me to the top of the lighthouse for a moment. There's something I'd like to see."

She suddenly looked rather rigid and tight-faced again, like someone trying to stifle a hiccup. "I'm sure you know the way," said Mary Bishop.

"I would never feel comfortable trespassing without your attendance," he said with a quick smile.

"The door to the tower is always open," she rebutted.

"And if I have a mishap on the stairs and injure myself on the way up?"

"The turret acts like a bell tower," she told him with odd breathlessness, as if she herself had just climbed the eighty-eight steps. "Every sound is magnified. I'm sure I could hear you sneeze, let alone cry for help."

There was a long pause. I could not say why, but that one simple phrase—"cry for help"—seemed to make him uncomfortable, as if it touched too closely to the reality of his heart.

"Are you searching for something special?" said Mary Bishop. People often came to the lighthouse to look for things. A lost dog, a lost cat, a lost child. A man once came looking for a stolen horse and carriage, which, after climbing the stairs and gazing out over the island, he espied hidden under a canopy of poinciana trees four blocks away. On the other hand, a milliner once wanted permission to climb the tower every afternoon at three, so she could see with her own eyes whether her husband was visiting another woman's house. Mary Bishop refused.

Her hand trembled slightly against the edge of the silver tea tray.

"I suppose I'm searching," the Reverend Neighbor replied, almost with a schoolboy stammer. All trace of laughter had now vanished from his face. He sounded wounded.

There was another, weightier pause.

He reached into his coat pocket and passed her a flower then. A small cluster of flaming red ixora. No bigger than a thimbleful—a demitasse would have been an adequate vase—but the intensity of the color made it seem extravagant. "I would, of course, have . . . I mean, larger flowers . . . but, you know, walking here . . ."

"There are always people," she said quickly, accepting the little head of flowers and twirling them slowly with pleasure between her thumb and forefinger. She looked up and stared at him, or rather, she stared at his beautiful hair. I think she was in love with his hair, she often sat admiring it so, gazing at it intently when he spoke.

"*Please,*" he suddenly said, in a very low, urgent voice.

She closed her eyes, was in distress. Her face was like the faces one sometimes glimpses at sea, of people on their first voyage (or their second or third, it doesn't matter which number it is), leaving home, sailing away in happiness, joy, distress, anguish—it's all the same thing, these feelings. The departure's the thing: the moment the anchor is weighed and the ship no longer touches any part of the dock. She sighed. The unwanted blush returned.

Fafner and I accompanied them out of the house, full of expectation, but when we reached the great iron door of the lighthouse, the door that led directly into the tower, it was closed in our faces.

We played in the garden instead.

It was only later that I looked up and saw the Reverend Neighbor and Mary Bishop standing side by side at the top of the lighthouse. The low afternoon sun spread a primrose light over the scene. No matter how airless and torpid it was at the base of the lighthouse, there was always a good breeze at the top, and so it was now. Mary Bishop held a hand to her hair to keep it from coming undone. She was looking down, her eyes averted from the Reverend's, and the Reverend was speaking to her with an earnest expression on his face. To an unsuspecting eye they might have been discussing a benefit drive for disabled seamen or a new window for the church. She turned her head away from him then, abruptly, and looked far out to sea. Her hand dropped from her hair. Several locks began to dance wildly against her cheek. The sun caught the lenses of her glasses perfectly for a moment, and there was a blinding reflection, a flash, from her eyes.

A few minutes later the two of them disappeared from view.

It was an hour or so later, close to sunset, when I saw Mary Bishop again. The Reverend was gone. Mary Bishop was running— uncharacteristically—toward the house. Her white dress tried to keep her from running. (Oh, what kind of dress it is that seeks to make a hostage of its occupant?) She was again pressing a hand to her hair, though to absolutely no avail, since it was all unraveled around her face in a great torrent of reckless, sensuous curls. She had a look of confusion. Her cheeks were deeply, unnaturally flushed.

She barely got the light lit in time, and even then it was only with Griffin and Ada's help.

SEVENTEEN

*M*y rolling pin is ready if you steal one more kiss . . ."
Boisterous music roared from the belly of the upright
piano, like hearty guffaws from a barrel-chested stoker.

"My aim is true and steady, and I am not prone to miss . . ."

The spirit of Mary Bishop's singing was infectious. Peer outside, and there was the sailmaker's wife across the street sweeping
bougainvillea blossoms from her front steps with an unexpected
blitheness. There was an old man on a porch tapping his mahogany cane to the irresistible rhythms; even the tail of the old
schipperke next to him seemed to flick in happy cadence to the
music.

"Old Moses had his Bible to scare away all sin . . ."

Mary Bishop's feet were brisk as she fiercely manipulated the pedals.

"The one thing I can count on is my faithful rolling pin . . ."

Of the house in which I now suddenly found myself a tenant, I can only say that what it lacked in dimension—it was tiny, to be sure—it more than made up for in coziness, security, and wide expanse of heart.

Dulca domicile, cato inquisitat, urged the Latin poet: "If you want to know whether a house is sweet, ask a cat."

The Bishop family was not wealthy. The Bishop family had no investments to speak of or squabble over, no shares to gain interest from, no inheritance—either present or forthcoming—to preoccupy or estrange them. The Bishop family had no priceless works of art, no inestimable and enviable heirlooms to fill their rooms. But the Bishop family had each other, bound together in the dearest loyalty, the deepest love, protective one of the other unto death. It was this spirit that permeated the little cottage by the lighthouse night and day, even when there was momentary bickering and a burst of transient tears.

"My rolling pin is ready, if you whisper in my ear . . ."

A parlor, a kitchen, and three small bedrooms were all the house consisted of. Each bedroom had its own private exit to the outside world, an eccentric luxury incorporated years earlier to give privacy to the alternating rotations of men who had once tended the lighthouse. And each room had its own tall and gen- erous window, protected by hurricane shutters. During a tropical rain, how cozy the rooms were, with raindrops beading noisily down the shutters and a warm, soporific breeze wafting through the soothing interior.

"Pray, sir, I tell you boldly, I loathe the smell of beer . . ."

The parlor was plainly furnished: a white wicker chair with a white wicker table beside it, quilted footstools, a braided carpet on the floor. And books: books on the mantel, books on the table, books neatly stacked on the floor, books about stargazing, books about sailing, books about faraway islands and the people who had visited them two hundred years earlier when traveling was still a half-mad and daring thing to do. Mary Bishop read to her children. Her children read to her and each other. And the parlor was like a cozy ship, sailing away—safely, briefly—to Martinique, India, or even farther, to the stars.

"If you go now without winking, I'll take pity on your sin . . ."

The parlor curtains were of gleaming white lace, the oil lamps were gleaming brass; there was a small sewing machine in the corner, and even its wheels and buttons gleamed. A gleaming portrait of the deceased Mr. Bishop hung above the fireplace: He was an educated-looking man, neither handsome nor ugly, neither convivial nor phlegmatic in appearance, but forthright, manly, and unaffected. He looked nothing like his offspring, but at the same time looked like every father in the world. He was bald, and the top of his head, like everything else in that room, gleamed.

"And you won't taste the hardness of my faithful rolling pin . . ."

However, one object in the parlor outweighed every other in sentimental importance, in the pleasure it brought its owner: Mary Bishop's piano—white, upright, a plain and unimpressive instrument by any standard, with a plain and unimpressive oak piano bench in front of it.

Oh, the afternoons when Mary Bishop sat and played songs the entire neighborhood could hear. In contrast to her often sober demeanor, she demanded robust melodies and giddy lyrics from a song: "And Daddy said no more dancing tonight"; "The pig's in the well, and we're all going to—blazes"; "The Havana Double Shuffle."

The rolling pin song had two more verses, which she launched into with the most enthusiastic vigor, while Ada and Griffin sat on either side of her and clapped their hands to the rhythm.

Then Fafner himself, driven into a state of irrepressible excitement by the song, jumped up while she was playing and began to romp along the piano keys, creating what seemed to him the most divinely inspired counterpoint imaginable.

Mary Bishop stopped playing. A fierce scolding brewed on her lips. But when she saw him dancing on the keyboard, chasing first a G flat, then his own tail, I was sure she would laugh. Her face seemed poised on the verge of unrestrained laughter, like a diver poised on the edge of a tall sea cliff. But then she remembered herself. She smiled. She shook her head, and lifted Fafner from the keyboard.

"Practicing for your next recital?" she asked.

He stared at her with big green eyes full of disappointment.

She gently set him down on the parlor floor, before returning to the rowdy strains of *"You better start a-running from my faithful rolling pin . . ."*

EIGHTEEN

a lightning whelk! Oh, Mama, it means you're going to take a sea trip soon!"

The day broke brilliant, as if a sapphire had opened and encompassed the earth.

Beachcombing days were the happiest.

The whelk, the color of butterscotch ice cream, went into Mary Bishop's basket to join the tritons, conchs, spindles, and other shells that had already been placed there. The shore was scattered with shells, which Mary Bishop carefully collected and put in her round wicker skep. The skep had been lined with a lace piano shawl to keep the shells from rolling too much.

It was a great mystery, the purpose of gathering these pretty shells: helmets, vases, bonnets, turbans, cowries, dove-shells, olives. Pantries at home were full of them, but they were never used to make boxes or mirrors, or to decorate candleholders. Yet the possession of them, even while they gathered dust and went months without being examined, gave everyone in the house comfort and satisfaction, like money in the bank.

"Where will you go, Mama?" Ada asked.

"Where will I go *when*?"

"On your sea trip," Ada pressed. "Will you go to Tahiti? Or Mauritius? Or Bali maybe?" She said this last as if it were one word—"Balimaybe"—a new place.

"There is *no* Balimaybe," Griffin teased.

"*You* know what I meant," Ada glowered.

We climbed over glistening rocks, into a southeasterly breeze, and ran across the small patches of soft sand that occasionally appeared, and then disappeared, between white coral boulders. The water, everyone agreed, was warm for the time of year.

"It's only a superstition," said Mary Bishop. "I know people who found lightning whelks who never went anywhere." The thought of a long sea trip seemed to rankle her just then. She shielded her eyes from the tropical sun with her hand.

The sight of our entourage must have startled more than one daydreaming beachgoer. Mary Bishop led the way, dressed in white; Ada followed behind her, in white also, but boldly with powder blue ribbons in her dark hair and a necklace of blue beads around her neck; then there was Griffin, and finally Fafner and me trailing in the rear. Fafner and I did not like to get our feet wet. But the surge of waves and the sound of surf did nothing to discourage us. There was nothing so unusual in the sight of a mother and her two children scavenging the shore and collecting gifts from the sea; but it was something else again, two lean and scruffy cats leaping behind them, bounding over wet rocks in the sunshine and struggling to keep up.

On good days, the shore was like a grand, if eccentrically stocked general store: old iron hooks (reduced by the sea to a consistency like charcoal), wood boxes, glass bottles, things tossed overboard, things lost in a wreck, trash flung into the sea by the islanders, trinkets lost from the pockets of bathers. One could collect a house key, bits of cheap jewelry, a scrap of hundred-year-old silver, and a beautiful nutmeg shell, all in ten minutes.

"I would go to Tonga," Griffin announced.

"Why Tonga?" asked Mary Bishop, after a moment.

"Because the king is a good man who keeps leopards as his cabinet ministers," said Griffin.

"You made that up," said Ada, quick to assault her sibling's flights of fancy.

Griffin blushed.

"Of course he made it up, dear," said Mary Bishop, trying to keep peace. "He *knows* he made it up. I think I would go to . . ." Just then a young couple came walking above us, in the opposite direction. The woman was dressed in pink with a yellow scarf that fluttered in the breeze, like a loose sail, behind her neck. She held the arm of her beau, leaned her shoulder against his shoulder, and laughed gaily. Mary Bishop watched them, looked down at the sand, seemed embarrassed.

"Where, Mama?"

"Where what?"

"You were saying where *you* would go."

"Oh, I don't know. We live on a beautiful island right now. Why, *look* at those beautiful trees up there." A grove of coconut palms swayed near the shore; the fronds took the light and sparkled. They were set among rambling sea grapes, with leaves like cupped hands offering color to the sky.

There was little chatter after that. Beachcombing is *preoccupying* work; its laborers quickly fall into a reverie as they walk along the shore. Not much of a shore, to be certain! For the island had no beaches to speak of, no wide expanses of pale sand. The island's edges dropped off abruptly, creating crags and diminutive cliffs, like a cookie that has been nibbled all around. And yet, that too gave pleasure, for the shore presented a challenge, it had *character*, was not a plain old predictable beach after all. The islanders were proud of their craggy, difficult shoreline.

Blue-purple jellyfish had washed up and were marooned on the rocks, their gelatinous bells moving with a kind of pleading anguish, slowly, as if blindly searching for the sea again and finding only the withering sun. Griffin picked them up by the ridge of their backs, which was not stinging or poisonous, and put them back in the water.

"Be careful," his mother said.

She herself had remarked many times that nothing on God's earth was as mysteriously beautiful as a jellyfish, once you got over your fear of it and learned to keep your distance. Griffin collected few shells—that was his mother's part in things—but he kept a watchful eye for sea slugs, sea hares, and moon jellies that needed a helping hand.

Ada eschewed shells *or* jellyfish, and preferred the lovely pieces of old blue and white china—small worn-down wedges of it— that the tide sometimes drove in. Broken plates and sauceboats and tureens. Shipwreck china, it was called, and was alleged to impart unusual luck to its collectors; better luck, hopefully, than had been possessed by its original owners. But then, too, some said it wasn't from shipwrecks at all, just junk from the big junk pile on an upper island, somebody else's want-nots.

The sea, which had been empty before then, all at once seemed to fill with ships. They glided out from north and south, coming slowly around the rocks and into view. A merchant ship, a Navy ship, a two-masted schooner with jib-headed topsails, a freighter, a small sailboat. Dolphins danced in the bow wave of the schooner, and everyone stopped to look.

"Where *would* you go, Mama?" Ada asked, standing very close to her mother as the ships sailed out to sea.

Mary Bishop sighed. "I think I'd go farther south," she said dreamily, as if uncertain of the course of her own thoughts. "Someplace even warmer, more exotic, more distant. I don't know. Someplace very colorful." She laughed. "Maybe I'd just go for a day to Havana. And you?"

"I'd go to Hawaii," Ada said instantly, with conviction. "Daddy always wanted to go to Hawaii. He wanted to see the volcanoes."

Whenever we went beachcombing it was never to the beach that Fafner and I had washed up on; Mary Bishop would never take her children to that shore, because "good men had drowned there." But an island is a merciless sieve, and loves surprises. Once, when I lagged behind the others and screwed my nose into crevices between the rocks, looking for I know not what—only to see, to enjoy, to experience—I saw a long plank of wood, wet and eroded; the tide had jammed it under the boulders and hidden it from plain view. It had the deep good smell of salt and wind, though it lacked barnacles. Peering down between the rocks, I could see the varnish and red and gold paint, worn now, washed by the waves at high tide, but not so worn that I couldn't distinguish those fateful letters

ESTE

which ended in a watery jagged edge.

I shivered, closed my eyes. The shore melted away.

When I looked up again and turned my head toward the sea, saw the motionless green-blue water, the sun, the flat distant horizon, I felt neither sadness nor horror, but longing, an appetite more keen than hunger or passion. I cannot describe the moment completely with words. It stunned me, weighted me, stirred me, and confounded me utterly.

NINETEEN

*M*ary Bishop would have preferred us to sleep on the porch.
"Go chase a mouse!" she commanded as we sat one evening, Fafner and I, by the front door. She swept the door open.
No doorman could have done it more handsomely, or with more enthusiasm for the task. "Mouse!" she repeated firmly, like a general directing troops to advance.

She waited.

We stared up at her.

Her left foot began to tap.

Fafner mewed at her.

She sighed and shut the door. "Spoiled already!" she proclaimed. And walked away.

In the late evening hours, after he had climbed into bed, Griffin would lie awake for an hour or more in defiance of his mother's regular scolding. He pulled us close to him, as if his contentedness of spirit relied more on us than on sleep. Besides, the nights were so hot, how better to occupy them—since sleep was elusive—than with playmates in bed. He stroked my chin, he petted Fafner's neck, he played, gently, with our ears and whiskers. We responded less gently, by gleefully biting his nose, or playing with *his* ears, one of us on either side of his head. When our escapades grew too bold, when his giggles became too raucous, his mother admonished him from the other room: "If you don't go to sleep soon, I'll put them outside."

It was a threat she never acted on.

One of his favorite bedtime games was "Life Raft," in which the three of us had escaped with our lives from a storm-tossed ship at sea and were sailing the oceans on a small raft (exactly the size of his narrow bed). Swoosh! Swoosh! Up the waves, down the waves. We had managed, of course, to salvage bananas and fish from the sinking vessel and were well stocked to enjoy a leisurely trip around the world, making friends with whales and porpoises and sea monsters along the way. Our little raft hurried past majestic islands with waterfalls; we sometimes stopped to pick coconuts or spend the night on a beach. Great island royalty, with giant flowered headdresses, came out to welcome us. But soon we had to be off again. Swoosh! Swoosh! And the climax of the game was always another terrible storm in which we must huddle together, Griffin, Fafner, and I; we must cling to each other for dear life. Sometimes the game was so tumultuous, so real, that Griffin stuck his head under the bedcovers. "We're lost at sea! Lost at sea!" he wailed with terror and delight.

"What *are* you doing?" his mother demanded from the doorway of the bedroom. "Do I have to put the cats out for the night, or will you settle down?"

"I'll settle down, Mama," came the penitent voice from under the blankets.

"Starting tomorrow, I'm going to get you some good *healthy* books to read. Sensible books. Books about mathematics. Books about . . . about architecture! No more adventure books for you."

But it, too, was a threat she never acted on.

We spent the long hours of the night cuddled in Griffin's arms, our limbs bundled with his in the most satisfying safety and intimacy.

And yet, a strange craving stole over me sometimes, as if a faint melancholy song had been stirring in my head all day long but only became loud enough in the middle of the night for me to hear its words. I snuck out of bed (why should I feel so guilty about it?) and sat—alert, listening—by the open window for a very long time. The house was quiet. The sky was dark. *If I held my breath, I could hear the sea:* a distant noise, as faint and beguiling as faraway wind chimes. I could smell the black waves, forever marching in, closer, closer, with all their life and mist and debris. They brought memories of La Esperanza, of Silver Beard and the Skeleton, of my mother standing on deck with the wind blowing through her whiskers—all of it, all of it, I don't know why.

This nocturnal restlessness emerged, I have no doubt, in part from a strong, agitating sense of my own peculiarity. How different I was from other kittens my age! Kittens who have known only warm windowsills, and regular dinners, and gentle playful days. What was one to make of a kitten, barely half a year old, who had already seen so many deaths and who had survived a hurricane at sea? What stranger seeing me on the sidewalk could guess I had seen the murderous lime hoarders of Cayo Dulzura, or the begowned transformation of *Estella's* oiler, or the rescue of a Cuban red hen in the middle of the sea? My own sense of myself alienated me from others of my species, and left me for all time with a vague sense of being at odds with my surroundings.

It was these thoughts that often ran through my head while I watched the lamp of the lighthouse revolve in its giant glass prison. I thought of mariners far out to sea; Middle Watch was ending, and Morning Watch would soon begin. From an empty quarterdeck at night, the first mate or the master would be looking toward the lighthouse—with hope, with despair, with boredom, what does it matter . . .

"What do you see out there?" a kind voice suddenly whispered in my ear.

Griffin had come up behind me, awakened by my absence from bed. He touched one of my paws with one of his forefingers, as close as a cat and child can come to holding hands, I think.

"What are you looking at?" he murmured.

We gazed together through the dark window, our heads side by side.

"It's okay," he said after a long time. "It will be all right. I love you, Mrs. Moore. I'll always love you."

And then he slid quietly back into bed.

Not long afterward, I pulled myself away from the window, away from my secret thoughts. I jumped on the blanket, and snuggled deep in his arms.

TWENTY

a palm tree is an exasperating thing to a cat. One can go up, one can go down—there is nowhere else to climb. No higher branches to explore. No gnarled boughs that reach like twisting roads into cool and shady green hideaways. It is like a flagpole, or a topmast. Still, at such a height, the sea breeze, especially when it comes from the southeast, from the islands of the Caribbean, is soft and hypnotic and smells sweet like freshly cleaved mango. And the view is often worth the ascent. There are few lookouts more satisfying than the heart of a palm tree. Though one must always be on guard against coconut rats, unexpected gusts of wind, and idle children with rocks.

Perched in the crown of a coconut palm one morning, I saw a

stranger approach the gate of the lighthouse property. I have never in my life seen such attire! If he had come down the street begging door to door, receiving one piece of clothing from every household—an extra large shirt from the innkeeper, ill-fitting breeches from the chandler, one shoe from the haberdasher, the other shoe from the sailmaker—he could not have looked more peculiar, more a victim of whimsical almsgiving. A dark green cap covered his head, but it wasn't much of a cap; you could "take a bulldog by the neck and throw him between any two threads of it," as they used to say aboard ship. I guessed he was elderly, so stooped, so fragile did he seem in his posture, so much at the end of all adventure and happiness.

A heavy limp stifled his stride, reduced him to a kind of toy figure, like a sideways rocking horse, tick-tock, tick-tock.

A group of children rode by him on bicycles, stopped, and looked back, laughed and called him names: *queer duck, rum one, fishy*.

He ignored their cruelty (or was perhaps oblivious to it), and concentrated his attention on the lighthouse, which he stared up at with a dark sort of yearning. He leaned against the gate, as if he had come a very long way and had finally arrived at the object of all his travels. People frequently stop and stare at the lighthouse with a brooding expression. I do not mean the quick, rapacious gaze of the sightseer (was ever a term more inappropriate, since *they* see so little?), but something else, something more: a look of romance, isolation, the sea, mystery, stormy nights. A lighthouse is, by its nature, an unearthly structure, and exerts a melancholy—nay, a *philosophical*—influence on all who come near it.

Mary Bishop was walking through the yard with a bucketful of pulled weeds in one hand and a small handspade in the other. Griffin was lying on the grass beneath me, and was debating the weather with a caterpillar. Neither took notice of him.

This old man (I confess, the longer I looked, the older he became in my imagination, until I anticipated a veritable wizened mummy beneath that shabby green cap) shifted his weight from foot to foot. His feet seemed to hurt him. Hardly surprising, given those mismatched boots. But he continued to lean against the gate, clung to it really, as if, having mistaken the lighthouse for a church, he sought solace here, an answer to all his questions, a balm for his distress.

A pattering rain began to fall.

His face, which had been obscured by both the cap and the angle, turned slowly toward me in the somber light. Something of my heart went out to him. It was, from what little I could see of it, a sad beaten face, as if the rays of the sun were nettles that had carved hard grooves in his cheeks and around his eyes.

I waited to see if the light rain would become a deluge, and when it threatened to do so I climbed down the tree, backward, with my back to the road. The stranger had now reached the same conclusion about the weather, and was moving on: tick-tock, tick-tock, down the street.

By the time I reached the ground, he had vanished completely from sight.

TWENTY-ONE

The Reverend Neighbor came to lunch, with a smile in his eyes and a basketful of bread and papayas on his arm. Mary Bishop boiled fresh shrimp for the occasion, and baked a tall chocolate cake with extra frosting between the layers. They sat in the parlor, uncomfortable with each other at first, as if they were twenty years younger, afraid to say too much or too little, afraid of seeming foolish, and hating themselves, at their mature age, for not being able to rise above such callow discomfort. The Reverend's eyes kept glancing at the portrait of the late Mr. Bishop above the hearth. From the now-faded smile in the Reverend's eye, and the odd look of guilt in Mary Bishop's face, it was not absurd to imagine that the aforementioned Mr. Bishop was an animate guest at the luncheon and sat in a corner loudly voicing grave suspicions that his wife was an adulteress and the Reverend her seducer.

"Do you think of him often?" the Reverend suddenly asked.

"In truth," she replied with a sigh, "my life seems like a dream. I can't imagine who I was or what I was about then. Does that sound silly?"

"I often think of my childhood in New Jersey the same way," he told her.

A long silence, the worst silence between lovers—discontented and born of paralysis—overcame them again. If a dancer on stage had abruptly found herself at a loss for the steps to her half of a *pas de deux*, if a captain heading into a squall line had suddenly realized his sails were set all wrong, there could not have been a greater sense of panic and impending doom.

Mary Bishop abruptly picked up the glass plate full of shrimp, covered it with a cloth napkin, and put it decisively in the Reverend's basket.

"We're going to the sea," she announced.

"A picnic?"

"Yes."

The inspiration reinvigorated them. They breathed a sigh of relief. The late Mr. Bishop was not invited to lunch after all.

They disappeared through a gate at the back of the lighthouse property, and the last I saw of them the Reverend's dark hair was caught by a sudden sharp wind and swept upward all at once so it looked for a moment like an inverted rudder.

They reappeared forty-five minutes later. The basket was now empty of food, so easily and lightly did it sway on the Reverend's arm. Mary Bishop laughed. "What was it the crab said to you? Tell me again," she urged. And he leaned over, the smile in his eyes having now blossomed into laughter, and whispered in her ear, until she laughed again and pushed him away, gently, pleasantly. "It said no such thing!" she cried. "A crab would never say such a thing, even if a crab could talk!"

They laughed, and then went into the parlor to say goodbye. I did not see them, but it could not have been a very lingering goodbye, for the Reverend was quickly gone. They did not go into the lighthouse.

A few minutes after he left, Mary Bishop came onto the porch. To my amazement, she swept me off my feet. She hugged me close to her chin while ruffling the fur on top of my head. "A crab can't talk, can it?" she said. "No, of course, it can't. He's an impudent fellow. Have you ever heard a crab talk? He's a liar. A wonderful impudent liar."

She smelled of chocolate cake and sea breezes.

TWENTY-TWO

$\mathscr{W}$ho is that?" asked Ada. "A beggar?" She peered through the lace curtains, and made a sort of "Hrrumph!" of dismay as she stared at the lighthouse gate. Her sense of decorum did not allow for unannounced visitors, especially during a rainstorm. "Or is it a salesman?"

"That's no salesman!" exclaimed Griffin with his head through the cleave in the drapes and his nose pressed up against the window. "That's Robinson Crusoe come home from the sea, lo these twenty-eight long years on Juan Fernandez's island—"

"Oh, you fool!" snapped Ada. "You read too much. It *isn't* a salesman—he doesn't have a samples case."

"Maybe it's a pirate," said Griffin. "Sir Henry Morgan or Calico

Jack! You'll look a sight less pretty with your throat slit from ear to ear!"

"Mama!"

I can see that morning just as if I were there now. And how could I ever forget it? The rain had started before dawn and brought with it a penetrating smell of sea salt and sargasso weed, as if the tide had reared up around us and flavored the air with a dark, sea-borne spice. The cloud-covered sky was as penumbral and soporific as twilight, so that every movement, every thought, every word seemed halfway between waking and sleep, of little reality and small import. A pear-fire burned in the hearth, low and congenial, enough to dispel the dampness of the day but not so great as to overwhelm us with fervor. Outside, the palm trees swayed in a hissing wind; the green of the ferns and the philoden-drons was so rich it almost anguished the eye; and the muted light made the red hibiscus (especially against the white entrance gate) twice as fiery.

The man at the lighthouse gate was the same forlorn creature who had been there several days earlier in his mismatched clothes. His clothes were *still* mismatched, except that a thick blue sweat rag, typical of a merchant marine, had been added around his throat. He was drenched through and through. His clothes stuck to him like scraps of wet wallpaper.

"What does he *want?*" Ada cried with impatience. "He just stands there, staring."

"He looks sick," Griffin remarked in a low tone.

"He doesn't move."

"I'll wave to him . . ."

"You *will not!* Maybe he's escaped from a quarantine ship. What if he has typhus? Or cholera?! Mama!"

Ada left her place at the window to find her mother, but Griffin remained where he was, and his look evolved from one of excitement and fantasy to a more sober expression of concern and sympathy. The man at the gate—how could he have aroused any other class of emotion? He stood in the rain, as oblivious to the wet and the wind as a lamppost or a carriage step might have been. He leaned against the hinges with a kind of searching desperation. The same ragged green cap covered his face. Lovers may stand in the rain to announce their defiance of the world, children may play in the rain to make sport of Nature; but a lone man standing in a deluge—he signifies nothing but empty pockets and a desolate heart.

Griffin held me up to the window so I could get a better view.

"What do you think, Mrs. Moore?" he whispered. "Should we invite him in for lunch?"

Mary Bishop came into the parlor with a dishtowel in her

hands, and Ada behind her. Unlike her son, who had no inhibition about shoving his face up to the glass, she stood slightly aloof from the window and inspected the stranger hesitantly through the curtains, moving her head from side to side to catch individual details one after another rather than all at once.

"He looks hungry," said Mary Bishop.

"I'll take him bread!" Griffin volunteered.

"He's a seaman of some sort," Mary Bishop affirmed.

"He has cholera!" exclaimed Ada.

"Oh, stop it," Mary Bishop told her firmly. She sighed. "I wish William were here . . ."

Ada and Griffin exchanged looks. Ada stuck out her tongue at her younger brother. Griffin rolled his eyes, shook his head, and gazed out the window again.

"He'll catch his death if he doesn't get out of the rain soon," said Mary Bishop.

"Should I run him off?" Griffin eagerly suggested, reverting back for a moment to excitement and fantasy.

"No!" said Mary Bishop. "Just let him be for now. He'll walk on eventually. They usually do—"

There was a sudden loud crash from the kitchen, as if a monsoon of empty tins and pans were rumbling through that part of the house. Mary Bishop turned in exasperation. Her eyes flared knowingly. "Fafner!" she shouted, well in advance of her footsteps. "Fafner, out of the soup! Get out of the soup this instant!" She raced to the kitchen.

The stranger, meanwhile, had suddenly unlatched the gate. He meant to come in.

"Mama, he's coming to the door!" Ada shrieked. "Oh, Mama, come quick."

Mary Bishop may have come quickly—with squirming Fafner in her arms—but the intruder, by necessity, took his time; his limp prevented him from moving with much speed or determination.

Tick-tock, tick-tock.

Water streamed glistening down the sides of his arms and the hem of his jacket. It dripped from his hands. He looked as if he were sleepwalking and dreamt he were somewhere else. He was not old, despite my previous assessment, not in the least. In fact, he seemed in his thirties; but worn, worn, ravaged, and belittled by circumstance. His every movement announced to the world his struggle to maintain himself within it. I could see his hair, only a lock of it now, protruding from underneath the sad threadbare cap: red, almost as brilliant as the hibiscus in the garden, merely a lock. And I thought to myself: He looks a bit like . . . yes, he does . . . he looks rather like *Estella's* cook . . .

My heart struck my ribs.

Every hair on the back of my neck stood on end.

It *was* the cook.

Dear God.

But everyone aboard the ship had perished. I had witnessed it myself, heard it said often enough, heard it repeated with sadness and headshaking: the stories in the newspaper, an auction of all items and personal effects salvaged from the shore, a memorial perhaps to be erected at some future date in the cemetery . . .

But it was him. I knew. Wrecked and thrown ashore, like the planks of *Estella's* bulkhead.

There was no quick way out of the house, though by God I sought one then. My own claws seemed inept to the task, and infuriated me. Having tried to claw the very glass from its frame in the parlor window ("Mrs. Moore!" came a unified cry from behind me), I raced to the front door, scurried forward on paws too small and too slow; but there *was* the door, huge, immovable. I pawed at it frantically. If they had not eventually opened it, I would have dug outward through the wood, I am sure.

"Mrs. Moore! Mrs. Moore!"

Mary Bishop quickly moved past me and flung the door open. In came the moaning wind and the rain; out I ran.

"My dear man," shouted Mary Bishop through the downpour. "It's a very poor morning to be out. Is there some way we can assist you? If you seek dryness and warmth, the door to the lighthouse tower is always . . ."

At the moment the door opened, the cook stopped. He looked not at me bounding toward him, but gazed at the trio in the doorway, Mary Bishop, Ada, and Griffin. He blinked his eyes against the pouring rain. And then sank on the wet doorstep, groaning and weeping.

"Oh, dear Lord," Mary Bishop cried, and ran forward. "Ada, get a blanket! Quickly!"

The cook lay on the doorstep with the rain in his face. His cap had come off and landed in a puddle near his head. The sweat rag around his neck was now halfway undone, and revealed a horrifying scar, recent and livid, across one side of his collarbone.

I could see his face clearly—had forgotten how benevolent it was, what a strange and beautiful face.

Mary Bishop stood utterly still. She was pale, her hands were trembling. She did not move. She gasped.

The cook opened his eyes; they were black, totally black, without any color or life. I had seen that look in wild birds, maddened and overcome after a storm. Birds who, by instinct, return to some familiar place, yet seem not to know it when they arrive. He stared. All at once, a cry erupted from his lips, animal, desperate.

Oh, cook, don't you recognize me? My heart felt as if it would explode. *Don't you remember me?*

I expected him to turn his head, to look at me with a glance of recognition; but instead his eyes remained firmly on Griffin, and then wandered to the face of Mary Bishop, bloodless and damp in the storm.

"Mary," he suddenly gasped.

A chill clutched my shoulders.

She knelt down beside him and took his hand between hers. "I'm here," she whispered. "Ada's gone for a blanket."

"Mary," he uttered again. "I have come back to ye."

The Castaway

TWENTY-THREE

$\mathcal{M}$ama, who is he?" Ada cried out when they had got the cook out of his wet clothes and into Griffin's bed. "Who is that man?"

"Calm down," said Mary Bishop. She was pallid and shaking. She carried the cook's tattered boots—if such deteriorating monstrosities deserved the name—in her hands.

"Tell me who he is. How does he know you? How did he know to come here?" Ada was clearly terrified.

"I said, calm down. Go rest. Take Griffin into your room—or, he can sleep with me. I don't know."

"Mama," said Ada, with gravity and fear. Her look and manner all at once pushed far past her years, straining for a moment into womanhood and maturity. "Is that man *our* father?"

Mary Bishop stared at her for a long moment with surprise, said nothing at first, seemed relieved, and sighed. "No," she said with great emphasis. "That man is not your father."

"I don't understand, Mama. Who *is* he?"

"We'll talk about it later. For now, take Griffin to your room. I'll come get him when I go to bed in a little while."

"Mama," said Ada, with a chill expression, as if the ghost of the Flying Dutchman himself had just sailed through the dimly lit room. "It isn't *time* for bed. It's barely noon."

Mary Bishop looked around her, fretful then, perturbed. Her pale face was even more colorless than before, nearly the hue of her stark white dress. She blinked in confusion. "Just please, for now, take Griffin into your room with you," she whispered.

The whirling storm continued outside the windows of the house. Palm fronds fell from their perches and sailed through the air, landing in the yard like small skiffs run aground. The house had such a stark air of being isolated from all its surroundings, it was like a small and vulnerable ship in a tempest. It would not have been remarkable to feel it break loose of its foundations and suddenly rise, sway, and heave-to. The overwhelming rain continued unabated on the tin roof overhead. Otherwise, Mary Bishop would have sent one of the children for a doctor, or the Reverend Neighbor. Yet she was perhaps secretly glad the rain was as thick as fog, for what would she say to anyone under the current mysterious circumstance and with her thoughts in such a muddle?

Ada went to her room, her curiosity still ungratified; but she returned a few moments later. She had a shy look about her, like a penitent pickpocket. Her left hand was clenched around something.

"I found this in his pants, Mama," she said. "When I took his clothes outside. This is all there was. He had no money with him. Nothing. Just this."

Mary Bishop expected perhaps to see a humble crucifix, such as sailors carry, or a religious medallion specific to some superstition of the sea: St. Francis Xavier, the patron saint of seamen, or St. Anthony, benefactor of the wind.

Instead, Ada unfurled her hand and displayed to the light a small wooden figurine. It had a captivating russet glow, the result of the wood—gumbo-limbo or casuarina—which was orange-red on the surface, but which carried intricate depth and undertone, so that it seemed nearly alive, like a rare and peculiar flower. The trinket, a simple wood carving, was rustic, and unfinished; its outer edges bore the uneven marks of the unskilled knife that had fumblingly whittled it.

It was of a hen.

TWENTY-FOUR

$\mathcal{M}$ary Bishop sat by the fire, but very grave in manner, as if absorbed in dark imaginings, and studied me for a long time from across the parlor.

"He was on the ship, wasn't he?" she suddenly whispered.

Ada and Griffin were asleep: Ada in her own room, Griffin in his mother's bed.

I lifted my head from my paws and gazed back at her.

"That's why you ran to him this morning." It seemed to occur to her just as she was speaking. "You recognized him. Of course. Griffin found you in the shipwreck debris . . ."

Late afternoon—the rain had finally ceased hammering, but the wind continued to blow in its wake, redoubling its efforts in the fading hours of day and lashing iron-hard drops from gutters and trees against the house windows.

She slowly rocked in her white wicker chair. Her right hand was clasped around the little wooden hen, and I would have sworn she once or twice brought that fist to her chest, with intense emotion, like someone in the powerful act of prayer. A pretty photograph album, bound in rough red velvet with minute silver clasps and an ornate overlay of pewter snowflakes and autumn leaves, was open on her knees.

"All this time you've been here," she said, "in my house—and you carried memories of him in your head. You *knew* him on that ship."

There was a long stretch of silence. "I haven't set eyes on him in eight years," she continued in a brooding murmur. "He talked to you, though, of course, when you knew him. I understand him well enough for that. But—*did he ever speak of me?*"

Her eyes filled with tears. "All this time you knew him," she repeated helplessly. "A cat. I don't know why it disturbs me so much."

She sat for a time, and her face, depleted of strength, betrayed little of her thoughts or feelings after that. Her glasses alone seemed full of expression, reflecting the flames of the cozy fire, though she raised her clenched hand to her breast several times again and held it there as if trying to push it through the flesh and ribs and *in* to her heart.

She spoke to me once more, to whisper, in a tone as somber as the approaching twilight, "Mrs. Moore, what have I done?"

Meanwhile, the cook—still alive, but unconscious, with a total absence of light or vigor in his features—lay in Griffin's bed, more like an imposing corpse than a convalescent, spread out within pale green bedsheets and covers. The bed was swathed in mosquito netting, lending an even more somnabulistic atmosphere to an already dreamlike setting. A smell, as if old, brine-soaked ship timbers had drifted into the narrow chamber, filled the air. His bones, I thought; as saturated with the sea as an ancient keel. Behind the netting, the man himself looked a hundred years old, at least.

In all the events of the morning little thought had been given to Fafner, last heard wreaking havoc in Mary Bishop's kitchen, and last seen rebelling against her arms, which held him tight, as the stranger—stranger, no longer!—began his passage through the lighthouse gate. I presumed he had, in the subsequent commotion, sought refuge in a quiet dark corner of the house, had perhaps scurried under Ada's or Mary Bishop's bed.

But, no.

When Mary Bishop opened the door to Griffin's bedroom later that afternoon, she expected only to see the cook lying in bed with no companion attending him.

She paused in the doorway.

There was Fafner, curled up on the bedcovers. He was snuggled in the crook of the arm of the insensible invalid.

TWENTY-FIVE

$\mathcal{I}$ can but feebly portray now the degree to which my ease of heart was unmade by the appearance of that frail figure at our door. Although it was only my imagination, it seemed as if all that had been gleaming and white in that pleasant house was now covered with dust and sadness. If mere objects could feel, then every chair, every curtain, every pot and glass and window seemed to stir, like me, with uneasiness.

A shipwreck changes the life of every man onboard, even—some would say *especially*—the lives of those who survive, for the dead are safely out of reach, and having been called to God, are no longer subject to the torments of this earth. *Better to be alive than dead,* you say, *whatever the cost or consequences?* Then follow the cook's unhappy shadow for a moment.

It is the morning after the hurricane. The cook awakens in the mangrove swamps. He is upside-down. His limbs are so entwined with a tree, he can scarcely distinguish his arms from its roots, his legs from its twisted branches. The mosquitoes have been feasting on his flesh. For how long? Hours and hours. He believes for a moment he is dead, and that this swamp is the entrance to Hell.

He remembers very little, is even uncertain of his own name. Every part of his body aches, screams out with throbbing pain, but especially the back of his head, as if he had been beaten, repeatedly, by vicious thugs armed with clubs and chains. There is a sensation, like a thrill, in his heart, but it is neither warm nor pleasant nor invigorating. It is stark terror, panic—and it does not pass, will never pass, it is his bride now. And like many another bride, it will nag him into a deathlike complacency.

His mind is so dazed he is scarcely aware of what he is doing or why, but he manages, by animal instinct alone, to extricate himself from the swamp, and begin the arduous way back to human society. All during these early hours of his ordeal, his mind is a whirl, images come back to him, they shock him, *physically* prod and prick him. The faces of his friends, drowning or already drowned—bloated to an extreme that it seemed impossible flesh could accommodate. The corpses of men he has loved, men who are familiar to him—these are his initial memories. Then there is the memory of his ship, shattered into a thousand pieces—the vessel that has safely carried him across hundreds of miles of azure ocean. He has seen its riggings and sails scattered by the wind and dragged to the bottom of the sea.

As he walks, the sun increasingly acquires an unnatural intensity, as if someone were burning a brilliant candle up against the tender membrane of his cornea. He winces. He flinches. He howls in agony. He cannot make the sun go away. He cries out again, unaware now there are people around him—they are staring, watching—unaware that he *has* begun to pass from one life to another, but not into the blessed hands of Death; rather, into that state of becoming an outcast, a freak, a monstrosity—he who was once so strong and able, he who could make fellow seamen laugh with pleasure.

His clothes begin to torture him. He does not know why. They were wet and sticky, now they are drying and stickier. The salt from the ocean is beginning to distill out of the fabric and forms a sandlike grit on every inch of his flesh. And worse, minute embryoes of stinging jellyfish, content at first to thrive in the tiny pockets of moisture contained in his shirt and his breeches, are now rebelling as their microscopic homes evaporate. His skin crawls. His clothes crawl against his crawling skin.

He finds new clothes. He does not remember how. The most horrible thing is, his mind does not become clearer with the passage of hours, it becomes more muddled, soupy, flexible. His feet hurt. He does not understand why. It does not occur to him that one of his new boots is two sizes too small and the other is two sizes too big.

The world of the images in his head—he sees a drowning cat, its mouth open, its fangs protruding; he sees a hen (but, no, that was earlier, or was that later, or was that just this morning?) castaway in the middle of the sea; he sees a friend's face (is it his friend the navigator?) sinking to a sad and horrible death—he is more familiar with these images (their lines, their smell, their color, their contour, as well as the terror associated with them) than with the streets and people in front of him.

He occupies his time, how? Walking. He is driven to walk, past the point when there are bleeding blisters on his feet. He often has the memory of walking in circles, of sometimes occupying one small spot and walking around and around in that same spot for an hour. He is not mistaken of that. When he is not walking, he sometimes occupies his hours by staring—staring at nothing, staring at something, it is all the same. A day goes by, a night as well, he is still staring, has not stopped staring, not even to attend to his most urgent physical functions. He whittles small pieces of wood: he does not know why he does this. It harks back to something in his youth: time aboard a ship, the Middle Watch, boredom and fog, he was young and strong then, a person—these are not unpleasant memories. He whittles the same things over and over again: a hen, a cat, a snake. Nothing else. He is unaware of the repetition; he merely sees a piece of wood and dimly thinks, *I'll whittle that into a bird*, just as if he had never had that inspiration before.

And still, there are the moments when he howls, cries out, screams. He imagines there are knives pushing into his eyes; he cannot breathe because there is stinging seawater in his mouth; he sees giant animals—humpbacked and black, not whales, something bigger, something much worse—opening their jaws to devour him. When he screams or shrieks or begins to shake, he is not comforted or dragged away by his onlookers, for how would they appease him, where would they take him? He is on an island in the middle of the ocean. An uncivilized island. And besides, the people around him have seen it before. What port or island does *not* have its small army of victims of the sea, paralytics, men who wander in a delirium, who hang between sanity and the dark void that is its opposite, men who have seen too much, done too much, drunk too much, who have experienced too much terror and guilt? The good *sane* people of an island have seen it before; the kind ones throw him a scrap of food, give him a cup of stale wine, let him sleep in the alley next to their shops. They do not know where he came from. Who cares anyway? This man, this creature—this former ship's cook—is traveling in the footsteps of thousands of seamen before him, on an endless winding journey inside his own mind, past wrecked ships, drowned mates, dashed dreams, nightmares of the deep.

T WENTY-SIX

W hite pelicans filled the sky, took pleasure on the evening sea thermals, moved like individual darners cross-stitching a blanket that rippled and twisted on the wind. Clouds parted; the setting sun struck the bodies of the birds and made of each a glaring pink pearl against the aquamarine sky. When the last of the sun disappeared, the pearls, too, slowly faded into obscurity.

Mary Bishop heard distant sea songs in the twilight.

A sailor's life's the life for me,
He takes his duty merrily

Griffin sat on the front porch and giggled at Fafner, whose eyes were fixed with breathless fascination on a small red ball that bounced, bounced, bounced across the gray planks.

> *If winds can whistle, he can sing;*
> *Still faithful to his friend and King;*

"Can you hear it?" said Mary Bishop. "It's coming from a boat on the water . . ."

The Reverend Neighbor stood still.

A horse neighing, the piercing laughter of a woman, a rooster (having mistaken the setting sun for the rising one), the sound of raucous piano music from one of the groggeries along the towpath: all this, plus the cutting wind—but no sea song, it had evaporated.

The Reverend shook his head. "I don't hear it," he said with a suitor's regret; he who was afraid of disappointing her, even to the extent of failing to hear a phantomlike sea song.

> *He gets beloved by all his ship,*
> *And toasts his girl and drinks his flip . . .*

"There," she said. But it was gone again, as soon as she remarked on it.

Whether distracted by her thoughts, or simply weak from the shock of emotion, Mary Bishop did not close the iron door when she and the Reverend went into the lighthouse. She took her seat at the bottom of the spiral staircase, where she so often sat sewing by the light that beamed through the clockwork weight hole.

They spoke in whispers. As I peered through the crack in the door from outside, I could only hear portions of what they said. The island wind stole the rest, carried away words, entire sentences.

". . . a good man?" asked the Reverend.

"Yes. Once. I cannot vouch for anything now. I haven't seen him in . . . But Griffin—you know. That same . . ."

"I understand," he said softly.

". . . didn't even know he was aboard that vessel, the one that wrecked during . . . How *could* I know? He had long ago stopped using his real name. Besides, they said everyone . . . I thought I would . . ."

"Did you want to?"

"If you mean, did I ever hope he'd come back . . . Yes, of course. But also, no . . . have been so foolish . . . afraid . . . stupid, really . . . But an island . . . it forces you to finish your business, whether you want to or not . . . It has its own . . . Life here is different from up North. Oh, you must think I'm mad." She shook her head. "But it's true."

"It matters to me he was a good man," was all the Reverend said.

". . . silly things . . ." she said. ". . . a difference of opinion, that's all . . . fewer choices. My life was planned. But . . ."

He nodded silently.

"You must feel I've betrayed . . . from the beginning," she said.

He shook his head slowly. "No. You haven't lied. I never asked."

A mule-drawn streetcar came down the road in front of the lighthouse just then, full of laughing girls in identical pink dresses with identical lace parasols. I could see Mary Bishop's lips move, but didn't hear what she said.

"Do you love him?" the Reverend suddenly asked.

A thoughtful pause. Only the wind answered at first.

"I loved him," she finally replied. "I loved him for the same reasons I love Griffin . . . protective . . . a strange fierceness. I don't know. Island life does something to you . . . changes you. You're barely one step ahead of . . ." She shook her head again. "I don't know what I'm saying."

Another strong current of wind whisked through the yard and sent a flurry of shivering cold drops—final holdouts from the day's long rain—onto everything.

". . . quarreled," she was saying. ". . . peculiar . . . life wouldn't work up North . . . We quarreled . . . sent him away. I said terrible things . . . our father . . . envy and embarrassment . . . My whole battle since I arrived here has been . . ."

They sat in silence for a long time.

"In all the days of my girlhood," she finally told him, "I never *dreamt* this would be my life, in this place . . . a lighthouse. An island. Palm trees. The sea." She took a deep breath. "I told him I never wanted to see him again."

A heavy cart from the nearby docks, loaded with enormous brown bundles of sponges, bunches of green bananas, and an immense turtle in a wooden crate, drove by; its driver and his companion waved their Panama hats, hollered at passersby, promised in bellowing voices to get "drunk as frogs" that night.

Mary Bishop was sobbing. The Reverend pulled her close to him, with her face against his chest. He stroked her hair.

"I have to go," he said softly, after a long moment.

"So soon?" she asked.

". . . the church. I'm due . . . Are you safe here? With him, I mean?"

"Yes. But what do I do? There's nowhere to take him . . . will get a doctor . . . But what do I do then? I could never just push him out the front door and leave it to Fate. Not again."

The Reverend said nothing, was staring at the far rounded wall of the tower. "Griffin," he finally said. A heavy blast of powerful wind shook the tree limbs and palm fronds overhead. "Like Griffin. He wouldn't leave things to Fate either."

". . . think of me?" she asked, almost in desperation.

"I'm thinking you're right," he said slowly, thoughtfully. "Living on an island, living down here, where there's never any snow, or frost, never any autumn or winter, with the heat and the sea, always the sea . . . Nothing here has any kind of permanence. I've done things here I never would have done up North. I've *thought* things I never would have thought up North."

"Such as?"

"You."

She closed her eyes.

"And the lighthouse," he said. "*Us*. But I wanted that," he said. "I wanted to live somewhere where tradition doesn't . . . overshadow common sense. I just never thought it would . . . so overwhelming—this thing, this . . ." He shook his head at the futility of his own words.

"Will I see you tomorrow?" she asked.

"Of course."

"But, I mean . . ." She looked down. "I love you."

He took her hand between both of his. "I love you so much,"

he told her. He said a few words I didn't hear. Then—"I've got to go," he said, reaching for the lighthouse door. I scurried away.

"Of course."

". . . in the morning," he said.

"Thank you," she murmured. But did not look at him. "Thank you for everything."

He nodded, but she did not see it.

TWENTY-SEVEN

$\mathscr{I}$t remains now only to fix in the reader's mind who the cook really was, and to illuminate the unhappy aspect of his relationship with Mary Bishop. For they were brother and sister, and anyone doubting that had only to look upon the temperament of the son and nephew—Griffin—to see the family legacy at work, like identical gears in a great machine. For it is as much in the *essence* of a person, as in their upbringing, to have not only an impassioned disposition to fellow creatures—as if we were *not* separate species, but all common passengers to the grave—but an uncanny *ability* to garner the confidence and affection of frogs, wasps, dogs, monkeys, whatever God puts in one's path. Just as God installs in the world people with a mind for engineering and agriculture and leading great armies, so He sets among us individuals with a gift to make soul mates of His creatures.

Both of them—Griffin and his uncle—possessed this charmed gift: to set at ease the temperament of animals. A snake that would eagerly bite one man would never think of sinking its fangs into their hands or arms; a wild cat who might enthusiastically claw one face would not consider hissing or growling at *them*. This wonderful gift remains, as yet today, unexplained by the growing apprehension of modern science. A proper accounting of it will perhaps never be made. And for all the well-being and happiness it may spread among God's most naive creatures, this faculty, this endowment—even when so much superstition has been eliminated—still draws the suspicion and distrust of those humans who do *not* possess it. For one of the seeming qualifications of the gift is that its possessors shall be at ease with every species but their own, and must often retreat and hide from their neighbors in order to find peace of mind. Three or four hundred years ago, Griffin and his uncle might have been dispatched to a fiery stake, burned as witches, or tied by the hands and drowned for a perceived consort with dark forces: now they merely rankle the insecurities of others, and precipitate more envy than hatred.

But why then, if the cook were her brother, was Mary Bishop so terrified of his return, as to gasp and turn pale, to tremble, and gnaw at her own emotions with anguish at the sight of him at her door, drenched and half-mad? The roots of their disagreement lay far back, and so the reader must come back with me to the sea, eight or nine years earlier. For when Mary Bishop and her husband sailed from the north to this obscure, hot island (so close to the Caribbean as to be a part of it in all but name, so far from the United States as to share little of its rigid temperament), when they moved to take up the position at the lighthouse, her brother the cook came with them. He had never felt at home in the North; his perspective and life simply would not work there. And like so many other men of free-spirited temperament, who sought refuge on the sea rather than face the constant discomfort of an ill-fitting life on land, he resolved to make a home of this uncivilized island. He sought a new and more hospitable horizon, like so many other misfits who have known in their hearts that their only chance for happiness lay in a distant place, a place whose unstructured and uncouth nature welcomed their eccentricities. Whereas Mary Bishop saw herself as departing for the islands with a purpose, she saw her brother as merely running away.

The conflict could not have been plainer. Mary Bishop at first looked out upon the island from a New England vantage point. She truly *believed* she could cling to the sensibilities of New England's frigid orderliness; she thought she could transpose them to the ground of this tropical island, as a gardener might labor under the delusion that he could transplant the native flora of Hudson Bay or Lapland and watch it happily flourish in simmering coral rock under blazing equatorial sunlight. Nothing, of course, could be further from the truth. For a tropical island works according to its *own* eccentric laws and axioms; the social contract is but a wisp of easily demolished fabric here, which the elements and the sea gleefully make mischief of.

That they quarreled, that they brought each other much misery—all of this was known to the neighborhood, for nothing is so facilely broadcast as a family dispute. One's neighbors may never know any morsel of one's happiness, of one's everyday pleasures and contentment (for contentment makes little noise), oh, but be assured they can recount every detail of one's acrimony, every cause and effect, every coarse and brutal word uttered in the night with the windows open.

Out of envy as much as anything else, Mary Bishop sent him away. She banished him, both from her doorstep and, in an impetuous moment, from her heart.

"I married Mr. Bishop," she told herself. "My life was planned. I had no choices. My husband died, and I had fewer choices than I had before. But my brother—he's off at sea; he can do any-thing he wants; he stays on an island; he moves on to another is-land; it doesn't matter what ship it is."

The old childhood picture album that she had brought with her from the North—increasingly, her only proof to herself that she had *ever* lived in the North—lay forever after gathering dust in a cabinet, rarely opened, and when it was, how quickly she passed over the pages that bore any portrait, any sign, any re-minder of her brother. She was not a cruel woman, she was not guided by an untoward and inflexible firmness, but she harbored bitter feelings toward her brother. He took to the island as if he were one of its native species, as if he were born there after gen-erations of natural selection made him perfect for it. This seemed to her in some way to disgrace their origins. Was it not fit and proper to maintain some aloofness in one's heart from the wild-ness, the sensuality of such an environment? She remained baf-fled by his nature, which is another way of saying that she was hostile to the same yearnings in her own heart.

On the day of his departure, there were no fond kisses, no em-braces to send him on his way; no tenderness whatsoever. He slunk out of the house like a thief in the hours before dawn, with only a knapsack on his back, new clothes to wear as well, a good strong green cap, and fine boots—and he signed aboard a ship that sailed that day for Barbados. He changed his name. He never wrote. He was in all ways a perfect exile.

It did not matter that, in the intervening years, she watched her own son grow, and came to reevaluate the substance of her brother's nature in light of the child that was her own. It was too late. He was gone.

The exile's heart so often becomes a hard and embittered one. But not so for her brother. He was in every way happier with the creatures of the sea and the jungle, and if he glanced back, per chance, once or twice a year, upon his roots, and his family, it was never for long. His fortune—not material, but within the *spirit*—was found and engendered upon the waves of the sea, and on obscure islands full of life. There was great *passion* in his existence: the passion of unexpected adventure, the passion of color, the passion of the sea. He hardly ever succeeded at anything, he was not even an inspired cook, but did the job satisfactorily enough (and with enough good humor) to maintain that position. But he *did* succeed at contentment. It was difficult to think of any man more successful in the occupation of standing on the deck of a ship, and looking out to sea, and *feeling* and *understanding* everything he saw and watched.

Difficult, as well, to find many men who had left, in the wake of their long lives, not a trail of animals viewed as soulless orna-ments, birds shot in sport, creatures tortured for amusement, spi-ders killed out of irrational fear, fish treated as unfeeling objects, cats and dogs perceived as divinely guaranteed underlings, but rather a trail of creatures not only saved, nurtured, mended, and adored, but treated, yes, somehow as equals, with more similari-ties than differences to their human co-habitants, guaranteed—as much as God could guarantee a man of the same thing—to live their lives in peace.

TWENTY-EIGHT

Within twenty-four hours of his arrival, we thought he had surrendered his life.

Ada—who had now been informed of the facts of the situation, who knew that this was her uncle Daniel, a man with whom she had had passing acquaintance in her early childhood—sat by his bed in the evening, while Mary Bishop tended to the lighthouse.

"Mama!"

"What is it?" asked Mary Bishop, running into the house.

"I think he's . . . gone," said Ada. "I don't think he's breathing."

Mary Bishop, gray in the face, leaned over the body of her brother, pressed her ear first to his chest and then, having heard no consoling sound within it, pressed her face close to his features. Nothing. A mirror was brought and held under the poor man's nostrils. There was no sign of life.

She stood then, a heavy look of guilt upon her face, by the bedside.

All at once, there was a great heave from the cook's body, as if some violent force from beneath the bed had struck him in the mid-region and forced his heart into action again. His mouth opened, and he took a great gulp of air. He moaned. But he never opened his eyes or gave any indication of returning to consciousness.

The vigil was resumed.

He lay in bed, very ill. The doctor—a tall, thin, elderly man— gave the opinion that though there were signs of malnutrition and exhaustion, there was nothing considerably wrong with the cook, physically; but that, in likelihood, the man's wits had fled, and having departed so abruptly, had left the body as quiet and still as an apartment from which the tenants had abruptly decamped in the middle of the night. He prescribed cool rags to be pressed against the cook's forehead every hour, as well as liberal doses to be administered of a brown, molasseslike composition, sold for a dollar, with the not very promising name of "Dr. Vanette's Health Extraction Syrup."

"Daniel," Mary Bishop whispered to her brother one evening as she took her place by his bed. She pressed his hand in silence, for she could not forget that she had once meant to desert him. "Daniel, can you hear me?"

The body was as unresponsive as stone.

"Daniel," she entreated.

Although there was every likelihood he simply *could not* respond, even if he had been inclined to, she took his silence as a condemnation, a rebuke. She was not so self-centered as to see his illness as part of a planned machination to torment her, but she nonetheless suspected she was the ultimate cause of all his misfortunes and that if it were not for her, and the division between them, he would make a steady recovery.

She consulted another doctor. He concurred with the first, differing only in his assessment that it was a regimen of various Korean herbs that must be administered daily, which herbs he would happily supply to her, at no profit to himself of course— wholesale—for fifty cents a day. How any of these medicants were expected to be administered to a comatose man so near to corpselike condition as to be merely a few short steps from the cemetery's gates, was apparently left to Mary Bishop's ingenuity and imagination.

But then an astonishing thing happened. It was in the darkest hours of the night when everyone else was asleep. I alone maintained vigil by the invalid's bedside. A southeasterly breeze, like a foretaste of summer, blew through the hurricane shutters, and there was the soothing rustle of palm fronds outside and a smell, like orange jasmine or lemon blossoms, in the air.

I sat crouched on the chair normally occupied by Ada or Mary Bishop.

The breeze set into gentle motion the mosquito netting around the bed. The only light was a soft one from outdoors, from the waning moon, interwoven with a silvery reflection from the lighthouse beacon.

I was deep in reverie, for the sight of his face, even so haggard and gray, called to mind not only a dozen memories of my early life at sea but ignited the same confounding emotions I had experienced that day coming upon a piece of *Estella's* hull while we were beachcombing.

Suddenly I was aware of eyes upon me.

I looked up, and the cook had, without my noticing, turned his head in my direction and was regarding me with faint eyes over which there was a peculiar milky white film.

He was breathing with great difficulty.

"I . . . know . . . you," he whispered.

He said nothing more to make me think he was aware of me or

his surroundings, but closed his eyes again. A terrible tremor passed through his limbs, and I heard him whisper an inaudible name in a voice so painful that to this day the recollection of it makes me pause in anguish. It was only later it occurred to me that the name might have been "Señorita."

He resumed his previous state, and I suffered gravely under the knowledge I could no more convey an intelligence of his brief awakening to Mary Bishop than I could have engaged her in a discourse upon the relative merits of "Dr. Vanette's Health Extraction Syrup" versus Korean herbs.

Mary Bishop read to him, first from the Bible, and then, on some obscure intuition, from a little-known book of eighteenth-century travel letters, the author of which had made many explorations of beautiful islands in the South Pacific, noting especially the unique flora and fauna of the region, and the incomparable physical beauty of each port of call.

"The cocoa-nut trees are remarkably high, sometimes sixty or seventy feet, with only a tuft of brilliant green leaves, and a number of bunches of fruit, on the top; yet the natives gather the fruit with comparative ease . . ."

Mary Bishop paused, looked up, her eyes settled on the view through the bedroom window, a wavering stand of brilliant pink ti plants, their leaves of such an incendiary color that any mere mortal who dared to paint anything a similar hue would have been laughed at and denounced for vulgarity.

"*A little boy strips off a piece of bark from around the base of the tree, and fastens it 'round his feet; then clasping the tree, vaults up the trunk with greater agility and ease than a European could ascend a ladder of equal elevation . . .*"

"Oh, Daniel," she suddenly told him in a low voice. "Do you know you have a nephew who's just like you? I was expecting him when you left—when I sent you away."

She swallowed hard, looked down at the book on her knee, and closed her eyes.

"He's just like you, Daniel. He cures things. He talks to creatures. He doesn't fit in very well sometimes. He's prone to wild excursions of his imagination. But oh, I love him, Daniel. And I've learned to love you through him."

She opened her eyes again and scanned the pages of the book to see where she had last left off, seemed flustered, could not find her place.

"*Since the introduction of Christianity,*" she resumed at random—then stopped as if lost again. "*Since the introduction of Christianity,*" she resumed once more, "*the use of flowers in the hair, and fragrant oil, has been in great degree discontinued—partly from the connexion of these ornaments with the evil practices to which the island natives were formerly . . ."*

Her face went pale—not with horror or unhappiness, but an odd sort of pallor, as if a peculiar inspiration had just passed through her mind. She looked doubtful for a moment. One could see the struggle in her eyes: It was nothing less than a struggle between what she had been all of her life, and what she must now become in order to save her brother.

She closed the book, gently set it on the floor by her chair.

She hesitated.

"Oh, Daniel," she murmured again, with regret, resignation— the entire span of eight lost years summarized in a single uttered name.

Then she stood up and went to the bed. She parted the netting with her hand, then leaned down to her brother's beloved face, and whispered in his ear, "You are going to live. *Live* . . ."

TWENTY-NINE

*M*y written story draws near its close. And I confess I can find no reason to keep from concluding it, much as I might like to continue on with it. The young do not think that the elderly long much for the past; they think we have risen above it, that we don't feel much at all. They are wrong, of course. Oh, what I would give to be young again. But the only youth I can still savor is to be found in these pages. . . .

I see the lighthouse—and there is the cook. It is several weeks since his recovery, and though he is not entirely firm in body or spirit, he grows stronger every day, both physically and mentally. He is showing Griffin how to tend the injured wing of a brown pelican, an art he learned in Aruba, from an old woman—The

Bird Witch, they called her—encountered on one of his num
ous voyages. His fellow crewmen said she had the Evil Eye.
night she transformed herself into a frigatebird, they whispe
and she flew above the mainmast to spy on them and curse th
But the cook recognized her as one of his own kind. She tau
him how to handle wild birds, and now he is passing the same
art on to Griffin. It is an odd thing to watch them together,
lay on the grass under the soothing shadows of a palm tree: F
though they are not father and son, it is like seeing an older a
younger version of the same person, next to each other. The
still walks with a limp (he will walk with it all of his life), an
mind still drifts away to quiet mysterious places sometim
where he goes in such moments, I cannot say, though I hop
to happy days aboard the *Estella*.

I see, too, Mary Bishop, much changed in aspects of he
She dotes now on her brother. She has brought back to life
eight years earlier she had rejected and sent away. She
tremble to take credit for his recovery. "I think it's Fafner wl
it," she often says. And truly, though Fafner was not the on
zealously nursed her brother back from the brink of death,
play his part: for when the cook finally opened his eyes p
nently on the world around him, it was to see, first of all, tv
ger and expectant cat eyes staring back into his. Fafner

relinquished his own vigil at the sickbed. And so it is what we have done—our cold, murderous, conniving species—for thousands of years. We are the world's nurses. We sit, and watch, and console in silence. I sometimes think we were born to it, it is our place in God's creation.

THIRTY

$\mathcal{I}$ couldn't be *more* astonished."

"Yes, it *was* a shock. But the doctor says it's only a *turned* ankle. And with a few days' rest I won't even need—"

"I wasn't talking about that, you fool! Look!"

A stranger to the island would have instantly recognized the two women on the sidewalk for what they were—town gossips—so immediately identifiable is the species wherever it alights and makes a home, from Singapore to Siberia, from Australia to Montmartre.

The one, an obese middle-aged woman with a monstrous neck, leveled a finger across the street toward the base of the lighthouse tower, where a slim, familiar figure was working quietly in her garden.

"Mary Bishop!" she announced, with a cruel laugh.

"In *pink*!" said the other aghast. She was shorter, thinner, older than her companion, but with the same fearsome neck and identical eyes, and a sadistic delight in her own words—the more pitiless the words, the more piquant the delight.

"And green!"

"And *yellow*!"

"And what in God's name is that *other* color?"

"I don't think *it* has a name!" the older one chortled, crinkling up her nose as if preparing to sneeze. She rummaged through her pocketbook for a handkerchief, but finding only a pinch of old snuff at the bottom of the handbag she stuffed *that* up her nostril in hopes of stifling her nose's impulses.

"It's incontinent!"

"Riotous!"

"How odd she looks."

"Yes, as if not quite comfortable with it."

"As if a *nun* had added pink trim to her habit!"

They cackled loudly, and all their hearty snickering finally ignited the one woman's sneeze, though she still hadn't found her handkerchief.

"*Too* horrible!"

"How *sad* for her."

"Oh, Lord—look who's coming to pay a visit," said the second one, trying, with noble discretion, to daub snuff off her lip.

The Reverend Neighbor was coming toward the lighthouse from the other direction.

The two women laughed again, with malicious pleasure. They walked off, though hesitantly, like stragglers at the scene of a satisfying catastrophe. The words "pink" and "yellow" could be overheard several times more, muttered between them with a fierce renewal of merriment.

When I was certain they were gone, I stuck my head out from the philodendron leaves in which I'd been exploring, and ran across the road to the lighthouse.

Mary Bishop—in pink, yes. And yellow. And green. And a striking shade of red. Her dress was like a muted tropical landscape, fluttering in the wind, loose about the ankles. A close examination of the fabric revealed palm trees and hibiscus and wild jungle birds. A crimson macaw near her shoulder was so vivid it might've nipped at one's nose if inspected too closely.

She was tending her tomatoes, pulling yellowed leaves off the plants and resetting the stakes.

The Reverend Neighbor smiled as he approached, incredibly handsome in his dark suit of clothes. His black jacket brought the avian darkness of his hair into more striking relief beneath the morning sun.

"Are you well?" he asked.

She stood up, radiant, happy. "Very well," she said.

"That dress is—" the maddening schoolboy hesitation overtook him again, and you could see in his eyes how much he cursed it, "so handsome on you."

She didn't reply. She blushed, but she no longer tried to brush it away with her hand.

"I was wondering," he said, "if you'd escort me to the top of the lighthouse for a moment."

As she turned to look at him, her eyeglasses reflected the sun, the sky, the white tower itself.

"Only for a moment," she said. "I have so much to do right now."

"It's important," he urged.

Why were his hands trembling so?

He reached into his pocket and pulled out a present. It remained hidden in his hand for a brief teasing moment. Then he showed it to her.

It was a shell, unlike any she had ever seen before. Tightly coiled curves shimmered with a mother of pearl luster, and so many spectacular colors were hidden in its depths it looked as if it had been manufactured in a glass shop. Brilliant colors alternated with snakelike streaks of dark brown, so the effect was like pearl inlaid with wood. The complexity of its details, the beauty of its lines, awed the eye.

"It's from the waters off Madagascar," he said.

"Where did you get it?"

"A ship brought it in. The captain is a parishioner."

As she turned it over in the sunlight something dropped out and fell into the grass. She knelt down, searching. A glint caught her eye. She reached for it. A ring.

She laughed in a carefree way. "A bribe?" she asked.

"No," he said firmly, with a smile. "An invitation."

A moment later they entered the lighthouse together. The great iron door closed behind them.

I never saw them at the top. I never heard a sound. To a casual observer strolling by, there was nothing different, nothing unusual about the tower. Tall and empty, with only one great purpose, to guide ships at sea—that's how it would have looked to someone walking by, who had no reason to guess the truth.

THIRTY-ONE

*a*ll that is left is to say a few final words about the individual fates of these people, whom I have loved so much.

The Reverend and Mary Bishop were, of course, married. And just as a bosun's mate had, fifty years earlier, taken the youngest Mobriaty sister from the sequestered life of the lighthouse, so, too, the Reverend took Mary Bishop away from the beacon as well. Though she can still be seen on many beautiful spring or summer afternoons, walking on the sidewalk in front of it, gazing at the leaves of the towering sapodilla trees, peering discreetly from a distance into the house, I do not think she misses it. She and the Reverend live in a lovely small house on Solares Hill, with peach-colored shutters and a garden full of heliconias and vanilla vines in front of it.

The Castaway

Her brother occupies the small house next to theirs. *His* garden is a riotous jungle, so densely packed with every conceivable palm tree, flowering shrub, and hanging orchid that the cottage itself has entirely vanished behind it, and strangers innocently stepping within to admire a flower can sometimes be heard a few moments later begging for assistance, they have lost their way. He raises and takes care of various animals in his house—his property is slyly called "The Ark" by his neighbors—but there is no hen among his menagerie, for there was only one dear to his heart, and her fate on the sea was too painful ever to be reminded of.

A retired sea captain from Provincetown took over the lighthouse. He, in turn, was succeeded by an adventurous young man from California, who brought his wife and three babies with him. He and his wife are there now, growing old together. The babies are grown and have lives of their own. I often wonder how long it will be, in this increasingly mechanized age of ours, before the work of the light is done by machines, machines by themselves with no human hands to assist them—or before lighthouses are completely unnecessary at all. I hope I shall not live to see that day. And, truly, it is unlikely I will.

Ada married a schoolteacher, barely a handful of years after the events related here. They live on the coast of South Carolina. We see her once a year at least, though not often enough, I'm sure. She takes her own children beachcombing now, but complains that the beaches of South Carolina are bereft of shipwreck china. Her most enthusiastic occupation, when she comes to visit, is to scour the same rocky shores of the island that she explored as a child, in search of those lovely worn-away wedges of blue and white china, which she treasures so greatly and which have brought her such good fortune.

Fafner, I am sorry to say, died not long after Ada was married. He had always been a somewhat sickly cat—it was nothing overt—it was just something about him. Anyone who has had such a cat will know what I mean immediately. He lived with the Reverend and Mary Bishop and Griffin and me. We played, oh so many beautiful days, in the garden. We had lovely times. He was in all ways my beloved brother, and I miss him so much, even now, after all of this time.

It was another ten years before *I* returned to the sea, as I increasingly longed to do. My life on the island was happy, with Mary Bishop and her new husband, but the sea does a terrible thing to you—you can never get away from it, once you have caught the fever of it, once it has bewitched you. Griffin himself became a seaman, first on a freighter out of Key Largo, then on a scientific vessel that sailed the Caribbean. He was very much interested in the still-controversial theories of Mr. Darwin; but, truly, I believed it was not theories that fascinated him as much as *life* itself, every aspect of it, every living thing. I accompanied him on his travels; we could never be separated. I was the highly favored mascot of many a voyage to many an island, and wherever we went we were made to feel welcomed and soon acquired a happy reputation—Griffin and his cat—in many ports of call. On one voyage I remember being on deck at night with Griffin as he looked out over the black ocean, the great somber expanse of it; there was no moon. There was a sudden splash—abrupt, momentary—from some unseen creature in the water off the starboard bow. "Life," Griffin whispered in my ear, "is the light in the darkness. It's all that matters."

And so I am still with Griffin now, in the fading days of my life. He has a house near the lighthouse, just behind it in fact, so that its beacon is a constant part of our lives. It is from that place that I am writing this now.

And when I finally die—it cannot be too much longer—I hope it will be in Griffin's arms, and that the last thing I shall ever see is his beautiful face with the lighthouse illuminated behind him.

Acknowledgments

Acknowledgments are usually reserved for nonfiction books, but are no less necessary for works of fiction. There are people who contribute to a book not only with suggestions and readings, but in a very practical way, in terms of clearing an open path for any writer to pursue the object of his literary desire. With that in mind, I would like to thank: Jennifer Dickerson, Richard Donley, Randy Fizer, Paul Hause, Andrew Holleran, Bill Jump, Kari Paschall, Eric Selby, Sam Staggs, Roger Striffler, and Stephanie Tade.